UnOpen Dream

UnOpen Dream

Patricia Lee

Printed in the United States of America

Publishing services by Selah Publishing Group, LLC, Bristol, Tennessee.
The views expressed or implied in this work do not necessarily reflect
those of Selah Publishing Group.

ISBN: 978-1-58930-277-8
Library of Congress Control Number: 2011915379

This book is dedicated
with love
to my family
and friends.

Acknowledgments

This story is what it is because of all the people who have touched my life. Each one has added a unique, special story that has enabled me to create this story. This is my second book—which is amazing to me because I thought I would be the last person on Earth to write a book! But, you just have to let out the story inside your head. I want to thank my son and daughter-in-law, and my daughter and son-in-law, who are loved very much, for all their encouragement; as well as my two grand children, Chase and Kier, who are my biggest fans; and my husband Paul who always supports me in whatever I do.

Chapter One

The sun was coming up as Molly and Gary drove into the town of Chicopee Falls. The temperature was already on the rise. It was going to be a warm summer day.

Molly opened her eyes to see a beautiful sunrise. It was so bright, she couldn't see for a few minutes. "How long have I been asleep?"

"Well, we were in another State when you went to sleep. And, now we are in Massachusetts."

"Oh, I am so sorry. Did you get tired while you were driving?"

"No, I was just driving and thinking about what our new life will be like here, and that I am so happy that we are finally husband and wife."

Molly reached over and put her hand on Gary's arm. "We will have a wonderful life here. I am so excited to be an Air Force wife."

As they drove into town, they saw a big sign that said, "Westover AFB."

"That is where we need to go," Gary told Molly. "I have to report to my commanding officer first, then we can go and find Nancy and Billy. They live on Lyman Street."

Billy was a high school friend of Gary. He had joined the Air Force a year before Gary. Billy and Nancy had gotten married right out of high school also. It was so nice to have Nancy and Billy stationed there too. Billy had found Gary and Molly an apartment two doors down from them!

It didn't take Gary too long to report in and get his papers and his job assignment. As Molly waited in the car, she was so amazed at all the Air Force men going in every direction. She saw Gary walking toward the car, and she couldn't keep from smiling. She was so happy and so much in love. Gary opened the door and said, "Come on! It's your turn now."

"What?!"

"You have to get your I.D. Card. All military wives have to have them."

As they were walking out of the building, Molly said, "That was a lot of red tape for just an I.D. Card."

"Yes, I know it is, but that's the military," Gary said. "We better get going so we can find Nancy and Billy's apartment."

Gary had read the directions, and Molly was looking for the street sign.

"There it is," said Gary, as he turned on to Lyman Street. "What a beautiful street."

The neighborhood consisted of big homes, and most of them were made into apartments. It was a very old New England neighborhood. The tree-lined street looked like something out of a book.

"I love this street," Molly said. "It is so pretty."

They had only gone about a block when they saw this big white house, 2206 Lyman. "That's it! That's where they live!" Gary pulled into the driveway; it went all the way around the house.

Gary parked the car, a '55 Chevy. It made it all the way to Massachusetts. It did well for a car nine years old. Gary had worked and paid it off before he went in the Air Force.

As Gary and Molly got out of the car, they saw some people talking. Molly was going to ask where Apartment 1 was, but she realized these people were not speaking English. They were speaking French. Molly had taken one year of French in high school. "Gary, those people are French."

Billy and Nancy came running out of the basement apartment. "We are so glad to see you! Did you have any trouble finding the base?"

"No, we did okay. The streets are sure different up here."

Gary and Nancy and Billy had been friends for a long time. Molly had not known them too long, but she really liked both of them, and she knew she and Nancy would be good friends.

Billy said, "Come on. Let's go show you two your new apartment. The landlord is over there."

Molly started for the car. Gary started for the car. "Come on, Molly. We can walk. It is only two houses over."

Gary and Molly were so excited about their first home together.

As they walked, Molly asked Billy, "How come these people speak French?"

Billy laughed. "Because they are French. Lyman Street is all French, except us Air Force people that rent from them. They are pretty nice. They take good care of their apartments; and if you can pay your rent on time, they are happy. These five houses here, yours and the four down the street, are brother and sister. Your landlord is Maurice Trudeau. He will speak English to you, but they speak French to each other."

As they walked up the sidewalk to the side porch, Mr. Trudeau was standing there. Billy said, "Mr. Trudeau, this is Gary and Molly Harper."

Gary put out his hand, "Nice to meet you." Molly just smiled and said, "Hello."

Mr. Trudeau showed them the one-bedroom apartment. It was small, but very nice and clean. Molly did not see the bathroom anywhere. Just as she was going to ask where it was, Mr. Trudeau said, "I will show you downstairs."

There was a door in the long, narrow kitchen that led down to the basement; that's where the bathroom was. It was all blocked off from the rest of the basement, which was the laundry room. For fifty cents you could wash your clothes, and for a quarter you could dry them. Molly was so excited that she would not have to carry her clothes outside.

The big old house had been converted into four apartments. They were all furnished. The military families kept them rented. Molly and Gary were so happy to get the apartment and to be so close to Nancy and Billy. Massachusetts was a long way from home and so different. Molly asked Gary if he had ever met a French person before. He said no.

"Come on, Molly," Gary said, "We better get the car unloaded."

Mr. Trudeau said he would be around the first of the month to collect the rent and told them where he lived, up the street, about a block away.

Molly and Gary began to unload the car. They had their clothes and several boxes, some of the wedding gifts they knew they could use. Molly put away the dishes and pots and pans. They kitchen was just a long hallway that had been converted. There was a refrigerator, a small cabinet, stove, sink, some cabinets above the sink, and no extra space. But, that was fine with Molly. She loved this little apartment. It would be their first home together. Molly knew, with some of their things, she could make the apartment so cute.

As Molly was putting the last of their clothes in the one little closet, Gary walked in the bedroom and sat down on the bed. "Hey, this bed feels pretty comfortable. Come over here and see what you think."

Molly turned around and jumped on the bed. There was a crack and they started to laugh. "Molly, you already broke the bed!"

They rolled around kissing and holding each other in their arms when they heard a knock on the door. As they jumped up off the bed, Molly said, "Who could that be?" As she was putting herself back together, she headed toward the living room. They had not closed the door, so she could see the screen door. There stood Billy and Nancy.

"Come on in!"

"We were not going to bother you two, but we saw the door open and thought you might want to take a ride and see the town."

Gary came walking into the room. "Sounds good to me, as long as I don't have to drive."

Billy drove around and showed them some of the sights. It was a beautiful little town with many historical buildings. There were a couple colleges not too far from their apartment; lots of little shops and places to eat. New England was so different from where they came from. There were so many different kinds of people and, of course, different kinds of food. Molly just loved it. She knew this was going to be a wonderful experience.

Molly asked Gary, "How far are we from the ocean? I want to see the ocean."

Gary said, "About an hour away. We will have plenty of time to see the ocean."

Molly said, "Before it gets too late, we better go to the grocery and get some things for the apartment. We all have to have breakfast in the morning."

"There's a small grocery store a few blocks from the apartment," Billy said. "We go there when we can't get to the base commissary. It's owned by a Polish family; real nice people."

As they pulled up in front of the grocery store, it was a busy place. Lots of people were going in and out. In the store, there were lots of foods Molly had never seen before. She finally found what they needed. They paid, said thanks, and headed for the door.

Molly said to Billy and Nancy, "I felt like I was in another country. I couldn't even read some of the names on that stuff. The Polish and Portuguese are proud of their cultures; and they live and speak it. I hope to become friends with some of these people; you could learn so much."

The long day was coming to an end. Molly and Gary were ready to get back to the apartment. Billy dropped them off at their front door.

"See you at the base tomorrow," Billy told Gary.

Nancy told Molly she would be at home tomorrow if she needed anything or just wanted to visit. They said good night, and thanked them for all their help.

Molly and Gary went in their apartment. Molly was getting ready for bed. She had gone downstairs to the bathroom, which seemed strange to her; but it was a nice bathroom, not too big. It didn't have a tub; only a shower. But she could get used to that.

Gary was getting his uniform ready for his first day at the base. He was a little nervous, he told Molly. Gary was an airplane mechanic, and he really liked his work. The Air Force had trained him for his job.

Molly wanted to make this a special night. This was the first night in the new apartment. She put on her pretty silk nightgown that some of her girlfriends had given her before she left Indiana. She had saved it for a special night, and this was going to be the night. She combed her hair and dabbed a little perfume behind her ear and on her neck. She couldn't wait to get upstairs to surprise him. She knew he was tired, but she knew he would be happy to see her.

When she got up to the bedroom, he was not there. *Where is he?* she wondered. She looked out the window and saw him walking down to his car. He was putting some of his things in the car to take to the base tomorrow. Molly finished putting her comb and brush and perfume on the dresser, and was giving herself one more look in the mirror when Gary walked in the bedroom. Their eyes met as she turned around. He reached out and pulled her into his arms. He kissed her neck and ran his hands through her hair.

"You smell so nice, Molly," Gary said, "and you look so beautiful. What a wonderful way to end a long day."

Chapter Two

Molly was up early the next day. She fixed Gary breakfast before he headed out to the base. Molly gave Gary a kiss and wished him a great day. She watched as he drove away.

Molly got busy cleaning up the breakfast dishes. She still had a few things to get organized. It was a nice summer morning. She poured herself a cup of coffee, walked out on her porch, and sat down on the step. There was another door at the end of the porch that went up to the apartment upstairs. She was anxious to meet the couple that lived up there.

As Molly was drinking her coffee and looking around, she noticed the large cemetery across the street. She could see a few people going for a walk in the cemetery, which seemed kind of strange to her. But, since she didn't have anything to do at that moment, she got up off the porch and started across the street. It was the largest cemetery she had ever seen. The head stones were very tall with all kinds of angels and crosses on them; very beautiful. As Molly walked slowly down the curved concrete looking at the names, she was amazed she couldn't read a lot of them. They were in French. Beautiful flowers were growing everywhere. The color and the sweet smell made her feel so calm; she kept walking and looking. She noticed a girl standing at one particular gravesite. She was a small girl, but Molly could tell she wasn't a child. She had long black hair hanging out from under a scarf she had tied around her head. She wore a long shirt, which Molly thought was unusual; but after all, this was a different part of the States. New England seemed like a foreign country. It was a long walk through the cemetery, but Molly knew she better head back to the apartment. As Molly was stepping onto the porch, a young woman in her twenties came out of the door at the end of the porch.

"Hi neighbor," she said. "I saw you all move in yesterday. I am Lagatha. My husband Sam and I live upstairs, right above you."

"Nice to meet you. I am Molly Harper."

"So, where are you from, Molly?"

"My husband, Gary, and I are from a small town in the southern part of Indiana."

"Sam and I are from Virginia. Well, what do you think of Massachusetts?"

"Oh, I like it. It is very pretty."

"Yes, it is pretty, but wait till the winter comes. It snows, snows and snows some more. We spent last winter here, and I thought I would never see green grass and trees again. But spring did finally come."

Molly asked Lagatha, "What does your husband do in the Air Force?"

"He works on airplanes out on the flight line."

"That's what Gary does. Maybe they might work together."

"Well, my husband has been in the Air Force for four years. He just re-upped for another four years. He plans on making a career out of it."

"Oh, Gary has only been in one year. He has three to go."

While Molly was standing on the porch talking to Lagatha, she saw the young girl from the cemetery walking down the street. Lagatha noticed that Molly was watching her.

"You will see a lot of her," Lagatha said. "You will see her walking in the cemetery every day. Her name is Helina. She lives a mile down the street on the other side of the tracks, if you know what I mean. The boy that she was in love with is buried in the cemetery."

"But, she looks so young," Molly said.

"She is young. I bet she's about your age," Lagatha told Molly. "I bet you're not much older than eighteen."

"I am almost nineteen," Molly said, changing the subject back to Helina. "Do you know this girl, Helina?"

"No, I don't. She doesn't make friends with anyone. She stays to herself. Her family is gypsies. They don't fit in too well around here."

"That is so sad," Molly said. "What happened to the boyfriend?"

"I have only heard the whispers, that they were in love and his family would not allow it. They tried to run away once, and they found them and made them come back. His family found him in their garage dead. He hanged himself. He had left a note that said, 'I won't live without Helina.' Rumors of all kinds went around. I guess Helina is the only one that knows the real story, and she doesn't talk much. But you will see her at his grave every morning and every evening before the sun sets."

"That is so sad," Molly said. "She has a broken heart."

"I better get upstairs and get some of my work done," Lagatha said. "I am so glad we met. I will see you later."

Molly felt so sad for Helina—to love someone so much and not be able to have a life together. How terrible for a family to keep them apart. And look what happened; he is dead, and Helina's life is so sad and empty, all because she was different from him. Molly didn't understand that kind of thinking.

Molly went in her apartment and finished putting her things where she wanted them. She kept thinking about Helina. It was still early enough in the day, so she decided to take a walk. She closed her door behind her, stepped off the porch, and headed down the street. Molly thought to herself, *I need to check out this neighborhood.*

As she walked, she saw a lot of nice houses. There were people out in their yards working in flower gardens and cutting grass. No one made any effort to speak or to make eye contact. So, Molly just kept on walking. She had gone about a mile; she had counted twelve blocks. From that point, the houses didn't look as nice as the ones on her block. *I guess this is what Lagatha meant,* she thought, *the wrong side of the tracks.* There was this old pickup truck in the side yard. The house looked kind of spooky. There was a woman hanging clothes on the line in the back yard. She was dressed like Helina. *I bet this is where Helina lives,* Molly thought. Molly remembered her daddy telling stories about when the gypsies would come through town you had to keep your door locked because they would steal whatever they wanted. I guess they didn't have a very good name for themselves.

Molly saw a sign in the side window of the house. She was trying to read it when she heard someone say, "What you want, girl?!"

It startled her. She looked around and there stood Helina.

"Oh, hi," Molly said. "I was just trying to see what the sign said. Hi, I am Molly Harper. I live…"

"I know where you live, down across from the cemetery. I saw you walking one day."

"It is very nice to meet you," Molly said.

"I haven't told you who I am yet."

"Well, I sure hope you do."

Helina just looked at Molly for a few seconds then said, "My name is Helina. I live in that house. That sign says, 'Palm Reading.' My grandmother reads palms; she lives with us."

Molly said, "You mean like a fortune teller?"

"Call it what you whatever you want. We are gypsies. And where are you from?"

"I am from Indiana. It is nice to meet you Helina."

Just as Molly was getting ready to talk, an older woman walked out on the porch and said in a very low voice, "Come in the house, child."

Helina turned quickly and went inside. Molly yelled to her, "I hope I see you again!"

Molly headed for home. As she walked, she felt so strange. *What a sad girl,* she thought. *I wonder where her mother and father are.* And she couldn't help but think about Helina's grand-mother being a fortune teller. *I guess she believes she can tell what is in your future, and she knows things about you.* Molly wasn't sure she believed in that stuff, but she found it very inter-esting. Molly hoped she would get to talk to Helina again soon. Maybe they could even become friends.

Molly enjoyed her walk back to the apartment. The street was so full of character. She just loved her new life. Things were so different in New England. She wanted to know all about these people and their traditions.

Molly got back to the apartment. The day had just flown. She still had a couple of hours before Gary would get home from the Air Force base, but she needed to get their supper started. First, she decided to gather a load of towels, so she headed down-stairs to try the laundry room. She had a few quarters. As she walked in, she saw Lagatha folding her clothes on the big table.

"Hi, Molly. Going to try the laundry room, I see."

Molly filled the washer, put in her two quarters, and started the machine. "I took a walk today, Lagatha, and I met Helina."

"You mean she talked to you?"

"Yes, she did. Not much of a conversationalist. She did tell me her grandmother is a fortune teller, or that she reads palms.

We didn't get to talk too much. Her grandmother came out and called her in. She was hanging out clothes on the line when I walked up. She never looked at me, but I could feel her watching me. Then she wasn't at the clothes line. But she came out on the porch and called her in."

"I can't believe she talked to you. She talks to no one."

"She was pleasant, but not friendly. I could tell she is so sad. Her grandmother did not want her to talk to me. I could tell that."

"That boy's family blames Helina for him hanging himself," Lagatha said. "They say she put a spell on him to make him fall in love with her."

"That's so ridiculous. That can't happen," Molly said. "You don't believe that do you, Lagatha?"

"No, I don't. But these people up here do."

"Why don't the gypsies move somewhere else?"

"They can't afford to. I think that grandmother has been here a long time."

"Where is Helina's mother and father?"

"They are there sometimes. No one knows where they go. They drive the pickup truck."

"It would be so lonely to live somewhere, and no one have anything to do with you."

"That's not the case for Helina's grandmother," Lagatha said. "She has a big business. The first of the month there are lots of guys from the Air Force base that come to get their fortune told."

"You've got to be kidding?"

"No, I am not. You can ask anyone on the base, and they will tell you she is a real good fortune teller."

Molly heard the buzzer go off on the clothes dryer. "I can't believe we have talked for almost an hour about Helina and her grandmother. I'd better get my clothes folded and get up to my apartment."

"Me, too," Lagatha said. "I got to get going. Sam will be home and want his supper. See you later. Have a good evening."

Molly said bye as she picked up her clothes basket and headed back upstairs. She could hardly wait to tell Gary about her day. Molly hurried and put the clothes away. There weren't a lot of closets in the small apartment, but Molly had a place for everything.

Molly got busy in her small kitchen. She wanted to have supper on the table when Gary got home. She fried some hamburgers and opened up a can of pork and beans. She doctored up the beans with some brown sugar and ketchup and chopped up a little onion. Gary liked them. She had a long way to go before she would be a good cook, but she really wanted to learn. Gary already knew how to cook a lot of things.

The door opened. She was so happy to see Gary. She heard him say, "Where is my beautiful wife?" as he poked his head around the kitchen door. Molly couldn't keep from smiling. She ran to him and jumped up in his arms giving him lots of kisses. "I missed you so much today. How was your day?"

"It was good," Gary said. "I am really going to like this crew—a group of nice guys. The guy that is my sergeant, his name is Steve; he will train me. He is from New York State. He has been here three years. I think he and I will work really well together."

"So, what's for supper?"

"Oh, we're having poor man's steak."

Gary smiled, "Oh, hamburger?"

"Yes, and they are really good tonight. I think I cooked them just perfect."

"They will be just fine. I didn't marry you, Molly, for your cooking.

Molly looked at Gary and smiled. "Thank God for that."

They sat down at their small little table that was in the middle of their living room floor. It was a drop leaf table that they used for a coffee table too. As they finished their supper, Gary said, "Let's put the dishes in the sink and go for a walk."

"That sounds good to me."

They headed out the door. Molly stopped and said to Gary, "Do I need lipstick on?"

"No, Molly. You look pretty just the way you are."

They started their walk.

"Let's go across the street to the cemetery. I want to show you something. I was here this morning. Then I walked about a mile down the street."

"It sounds like you checked out this place today."

"Oh, I did. I met Lagatha. She lives upstairs. Her husband is Sam. They are from Virginia."

"Hold on a minute. It sounds like you had a busy day."

"Oh, I did. Let me tell you about the gypsy girl."

"What are you talking about?"

"She lives way down the street." Molly was talking a mile a minute.

Gary started to laugh. "Slow down, honey. We have two years to live here. You don't have to find out everything in one day. How did you have time to fix supper?"

"It was hard, but I worked it in," Molly said, laughing. "I guess it can wait till another time."

Gary put his hand in hers, and they walked and watched the sun go down.

Chapter Three

A few weeks passed. Molly and Gary were settled in their apartment. They spent a lot of time with Billy and Nancy. The summer was very pleasant—not real hot and humid like back home. Molly and Lagatha would have coffee a lot of times in the morning. Nancy had taken a job, so Molly didn't see her during the week. Molly was still trying to be friends with Helina, but not much was happening.

Molly was having her coffee and reading the newspaper when Lagatha came out on the porch. "Hey, what are you doing? Looking for a job?"

"No, not really, but I might get one. We could always use the extra money."

"They are looking for help up at the college."

"I don't think I am college material," Molly laughed. "What kind of help? Like teachers?"

"No, they need help in the bookstore getting the books ready for the fall classes when the girls come back to college."

"Oh, what about the boys?"

"There are no boys, Molly. It's an all-girls college—

Mount Holyoke College. It's very Ivy League. The girls there are probably from very well-to-do families from all over the States and in New England."

"How do you know so much about it, Lagatha?"

"I worked there last fall. It is only a mile away. I walked to work; the pay was good. I only worked a half a day, about four days a week. You might want to check it out."

"Thanks, Lagatha. I will talk to Gary about it."

The next morning Molly got Gary's breakfast ready. She kissed him goodbye as he headed out the door to the base. As he was leaving, Gary said, "Don't run off with the gypsies today, Molly." He started laughing.

"That's not funny. I want to tell you about them as soon as you will take time to listen."

"Okay, sweetheart. Tonight you can tell me all about it."

"Great, I can hardly wait till I see you tonight."

"Have a good day, Molly."

"I will."

Gary blew her a kiss as he drove out of the driveway.

It was still very early. The sun was not all the way up. As Molly cleared away the breakfast dishes and started filling up the sink to get them washed, she couldn't keep from thinking about those gypsies. *What a different life they have. And poor Helina. So sad. I have got to find a way to be her friend,* she thought. She started daydreaming about talking to her. *Maybe I'll tell her I am part gypsy. No, she would know that was a lie. I know, I'll tell her I want her grandmother to read my palm. That's it! Then, I can see what their family is like.*

As Molly finished her work in the apartment, she started to get herself dressed and do her hair. *I am just going to take a walk down to that house, knock on the door, and ask to have my* palm read. I hope Gary won't get mad. But I just got to do this. So, out the door she went.

It was still early, but everyone seemed to be working in their yards or hanging out their clothes. Only Air Force people would speak. The French people, most of the time, would not even look your way. As Molly got close to that big old house, she started to get very nervous, maybe even a little scared, but she just bit her lip and kept on walking. She got to the front of the yard and she saw Helina feeding the big black cat. It was a strange looking cat. Its tail was half white.

Helina looked up and saw Molly. "Hi, Helina. It is a beautiful morning. Don't you think? "

"Yes, I guess."

"Can I come in the yard?" Molly asked, as she was already walking up the sidewalk.

"What do you want, girl?"

"Well, I have a name. It is Molly, and I want to see your grandmother. I want my palm read."

Helina just looked at her for a minute like she was looking through her.

"Do you even know what you are asking for?"

"Yes, I do. She will tell me about my future."

"Okay, whatever you want. I guess you think she will tell you that your life will be perfect. You know, she tells the dark side too. Molly felt scared for a minute. She didn't really understand the dark side, but she knew she was too far in to leave. So, in the house she went with Helina.

As the front door closed behind them, Molly felt her heart come up in her throat. She swallowed hard trying not to look scared. They walked down a hallway. The walls were painted a drab green color. There were a few straight-back chairs against the wall. They came to a door. Helina knocked on it. A voice from the other side said, "Come in, please."

The door opened. Helina stepped aside and told Molly to go in. As she went in, there was Helina's grandmother sitting at a round table. She was a small woman. Her hair was covered with a scarf. It looked like her hair had once been black. There was quite a lot of grey in the hair outside the scarf. Her face had once been pretty, but the years had added some wrinkles. Helina's grandmother was looking down at the table without raising her head up. She looked up with her eyes and said, "Please, sit down." Molly started to talk and the gypsy woman raised her hand and said, "Don't speak."

Molly was in the chair, afraid to say anything. "So, you're the girl Helina has told me about."

Molly just sat there, afraid to talk.

"You live up the street across from the cemetery."

"Yes, I do."

"Please let me see your hands."

Molly put her hands on the table.

"Please turn your palms up."

Molly did as she said. The old woman touched Molly's hands, looking at them like she could see through them.

"You and Helina are the same age, I see. You come from a large family. You have a good life. You have a long life ahead of you."

Molly was thinking to herself that anyone could say this. Then, the old woman said, "Your father is not your father. Your dream that you have over and over will not open. You can't finish the dream. The man swinging the little girl is closer than you think."

Molly jumped up.

"That's enough!" she said, and ran out the door. Helina grabbed her arm. Molly threw two rolled-up dollars at Helina and kept on running up the street. She didn't stop till she got to her apartment. She unlocked the door and hurried inside. She sat down on the sofa, trying to figure out what had just happened. How did Helina's grandmother know about her dream? Molly hadn't told anyone, not even Gary.

Molly held onto her chest. Her heart was beating so fast. She felt like it was going to come out of her chest. How did she know about her dream? About the man swinging the little girl? Your father is not your father? That couldn't have been just a good guess. Molly never even thought about Warren being her real father. Richard Preston was her father. She loved him. She never knew any difference, even though his blood didn't run in her veins. He was still her father. For some reason, she had been having this dream. It was driving her crazy. She was going to have to tell Gary about it. He knew she was having some bad dreams. She would wake up in the middle of the night. She would sit up in bed and would have a hard time going back to sleep.

Four

A few days passed, and Molly had still not told Gary about going to see Helina's grandmother. She told him about the job at the college. He said if she wanted to check it out, it was all right with him.

Another Monday rolled around, as the summer was coming to an end. She thought they probably would be hiring the people for the bookstore for the fall classes. Lagatha said she would be happy to walk up to the college with her on Wednesday if she wanted to go check it out.

Molly got up with Gary on Wednesday morning and got dressed. She put on her black skirt and blouse. She tried to look a little older than her age, since she was younger or at least the same age as some of these college girls. She let Gary out the door, finished putting on her makeup, and combed her hair. There was a knock on the door, so she went to get it. "Come on in, Lagatha. Want a cup of coffee before we go?"

"No, I had two cups already with Sam before he went to the base."

"How do I look?"

"You look just fine, except you will need a sweater. We have to walk several blocks, and fall is in the air. It comes early in New England with winter close behind."

Molly and Lagatha headed out the door. As they walked, they talked. Molly and Lagatha had become good friends. They reached the college. The big campus covered a couple miles. Molly had never been on a college campus before. There didn't seem to be a lot going on. There were a few cars with lots of stuff packed in them. A few girls were moving in the dormitory. There were about two weeks before classes started.

Lagatha showed Molly which building to go in. Molly headed in. She saw a sign that pointed to the bookstore. There was a middle-aged lady in the bookstore opening up a box. She turned around and saw Molly and said, "Registration isn't until next week, and it is in the East building."

"Oh, I'm not here for that. I am here about the job in the bookstore."

"Oh, I am sorry. You look like you should be a student."

"No, I'm not a student; just looking for a job. I am Molly Harper."

"Well, nice to meet you, Molly. I am Alice Pratt. I run this bookstore. So, I guess you are here to see me. I have already hired one lady to work full time. Would you be interested in a couple days a week?"

"Yes, Ma'am. I would."

"Do you know anything about a bookstore?"

"I worked in my bookstore in high school."

"And, how long ago was that?"

"A couple years ago."

"Could you be here Friday?"

"Yes, I could."

"The bookstore opens at eight o'clock." She handed Molly a form to fill out.

When Molly handed it back to her, she read it over very fast. "Does everyone in Indiana have that accent?"

"Yes, I guess they do. We're from Southern Indiana."

Mrs. Pratt laughed. "You sound like you're from Tennessee or Georgia."

"Well," Molly explained, "we do live on the Ohio River, which is across from Kentucky. I guess that is where it comes from."

Mrs. Pratt thanked Molly and said, "I look forward to seeing you on Friday."

Molly headed out of the building. She was looking around for Lagatha when she heard her say, "Did you get the job?"

Molly turned around to see where Lagatha was. She was sitting down by a huge tree. "What are you doing down there?"

"I was just watching the people and wondering why in the world, if you had the money and the brains to get to go to college, why you would pick an all-girls school."

Molly laughed. "I guess their parents want to make sure they study instead of running after the boys."

"I guess so," Lagatha said. "But, there are plenty of boys over at the college across town. I am sure they get together."

"I start the job on Friday," Molly said. "Just Wednesdays and Fridays, and only for a month."

"That's good."

"Why do you say that, Lagatha?"

"Well, in about a month we will start getting some cold weather. They usually have snow by October and it will be a cold walk for you."

As they started their walk back to the apartment house, Molly told Lagatha about her visit to see Helina's grandmother.

"You mean you let her read your palm? Weren't you afraid?"

"Well, yes, I was."

"What did she tell you?"

"I ran out before she finished, but she said something that no one knows about but me. I haven't even told Gary yet."

"What was it, Molly?"

"I can't tell you. It was really strange. You know they say things that could apply to a lot of people."

"This wasn't like that. I felt like she saw right into my soul. I felt like I did something wrong."

"Oh, Molly, don't be silly. I don't think God would be upset with you."

"I sure hope not."

Five

A week passed, and Molly liked working in the bookstore. Alice Pratt was a nice lady to work for, even if she did make fun of the way Molly talked.

Molly finally got up the nerve to tell her she thought the people in Massachusetts really sounded strange. "You even have different names for things," she said.

Mrs. Pratt just laughed. "Well, I guess we both will learn something from each other." Alice Pratt said she hoped to see Molly next fall.

The weeks were passing quickly, and the weather was changing. The fall color was just beautiful. Molly and Gary would drive around on the weekend when Gary was off at the base. Nancy and Billy would go with them. It was a fun time. Molly had never seen such beautiful country. Billy and Nancy had taken them to a place to eat called the Clam Shack. Molly had never heard of anyone eating fried clams, but she liked them.

Molly and Gary had met a lot of people. Military people are like your family. They look out for each other. They are all you have when you are so far away from home.

Molly continued to have her same dream. At least once a month, the dream would come back.

Winter was coming fast, and it was getting cold. Molly and Gary had been over at Nancy and Billy's playing cards. As they were walking back to the apartment, Molly said, "Gary, I need to tell you something. I wanted to tell you about the gypsy girl, Helina."

"You told me about her boyfriend hanging himself because they were in love and couldn't be together. What else is there to tell?"

"Well, her grandmother is a palm reader."

"I know that. I have heard the guys at the base talk about her. They say she's really good, if you believe that stuff."

"I wanted to tell you before now, but I got the job at the college. Then, I just never got around to it. I went to see Helina's grandmother. I thought if I showed Helina that I liked her grandmother, she might want to be friends. But, it didn't work out that way. Her grandmother read my palm. It was so frightening. She told me about my dream. I never even told you about it. She knew about my dream, and she said, 'Your father is not your father,' and 'he's closer than you think.'"

Molly just burst into tears. The tears were running down her cheek and the cold wind was blowing. Gary wrapped his arms around Molly, and they hurried into the apartment. Molly was so upset.

"Molly, it's okay," Gary said. "Those people just guess at that stuff. She was just lucky that she hit on it."

They got out of their winter coats. "Let's go get in bed and get warm and talk about this."

Gary got the extra blanket out of the closet. Molly had calmed down.

"Do you want to tell me about the dream, Molly? Maybe if you tell it, it will go away."

"I think the dream is about Warren. There is this little girl on a swing, and this man is swinging her. But, when she looks at him, he doesn't have a face. Then he just disappears. Then, I am walking toward this man and he has his hand out and a smile. That's all I see. Then I can't get to him. It won't get out of my head. Why would I dream of a man I have never seen and is dead?"

"I don't know, Molly, but I am sure it will go away."

"You know I love my daddy. He is the only father I ever wanted."

"I know, Molly. Maybe it's the unknown that's the problem." Gary pulled her close to him. "Close your eyes, sweetheart, and go to sleep. I love you. Only good dreams tonight."

Six

Weeks passed, and colorful leaves were falling off the trees fast. It would not be long before winter would come. Molly had not dreamed about Warren for a while. The job at the college was over. Gary had been working overtime at the base.

Molly was a little homesick. She was hoping to get a letter from home. Her sister, Lilly, was good about writing and letting her know what was going on at home. Molly knew she would really miss her family at Christmas. They always had a big Christmas for their family with lots of good food and family fun. Molly was amazed at what her parents did for their large family. They sure knew how to manage their money.

The afternoon had come around fast. Molly went to check the mailbox. She was so excited to see a letter from home. It was from her daddy. She could tell by his handwriting. She hurried in the apartment, as there was a chill in the air. She opened the letter and started to read:

Dear Molly,

Hope this finds you well. Your mother sends her love. Your sisters are well. I guess it is cold up there by now? We are getting rain. Tell Gary hi. Write when you can.

Your Dad,

Richard Preston

With a tear in her eye and a smile on her face, Molly knew there was a lot of love in that letter, even if he didn't write it down. Molly knew her daddy loved her. Molly sat there holding the letter next to her heart thinking how lucky she was that her daddy had come into her mother's life. Surely God must have put him in her mother's life to take care of them. Molly had never really wanted to know anything about Warren; but since these dreams had started, she really felt like she needed to find out about him.

Molly put the letter away and went to the kitchen to fix some supper for Gary. He would be home soon. She knew he would be tired and hungry; twelve hours is a long day. There wasn't a whole lot to fix; it was the end of the month. They always ate better the first of the month. There wasn't a lot of money being in the Air Force, but she loved it. She and Gary were very much in love.

She heard the door open; Molly ran to see her husband. He looked tired, but he gave her a big hug and kiss and said, "Tell me, my sweet wife, did you fix T-bone steaks for supper? That's what I really want."

"Yes, I did, but it looks like fried bologna, green beans, and Kool-Aid to drink."

Gary headed to the sink to wash up. Molly put the food on the table. They prayed and started to eat. They both laughed as they cut up their fried bologna. "We will have steak the next time."

Molly and Gary woke up early the next morning. They could hear the wind blowing. It was cold in the apartment. Gary jumped out of bed to go check the heater. They didn't know a lot about that radiator heat. "It seems to be working," Gary told Molly. "It must have really gotten cold during the night. I guess this is the beginning of the bitter cold winter everyone talks about."

Gary told Molly to go look outside. Molly raised the window shade and, to her surprise, it was snowing big flakes.

"Oh, my goodness. It looks like winter is here."

Gary walked over to turn on the radio. He heard the man on the other end say winter has arrived.

"We could get a foot of snow before this comes to an end tonight, and the temperature is 15 degrees with a wind chill of about 5 degrees. I didn't know it could really get that cold."

Gary laughed at her. "It will feel like 0 degrees on that flight line tonight when I am working."

"Oh, that's right. You have to work that late shift. I hate that."

"We better get on some warm clothes and see if we can get to the base and get my check, so we can go to the commissary and get some food in the apartment. If we get snowed-in, we better have some food."

Molly was getting her clothes on when Gary came back in the room. Be sure and put on your boots. The Air Force provided Gary with winter gear, so he was ready for the cold. As they walked to the car, Molly looked up at Gary and said, "This is our first snowy winter day in Massachusetts, and I love it!"

As they were driving out of the driveway, Molly could see Helina going into the cemetery.

"Oh, my. Nothing keeps her away," she told Gary.

"Have you talked to Helina since that day you had your palm read?"

"No. She probably thinks I'm crazy, since I left so fast."

By the time they got to the base, the snow was really coming down. The road crews were busy trying to keep the snow off the roads. Gary picked up his check, and they hurried to the commissary. They would cash his check for him. They got everything they needed, plus a few extras. Molly wanted to go to the base exchange if they had time. They had everything in there from jewelry to clothes, and the prices were really great. It was the next building over, so they put the groceries in the car and headed to the base exchange.

Molly couldn't wait to check out the jewelry. Gary stopped to talk to a couple guys he worked with. As Molly was admiring the rings, the lady behind the counter said, "May I help you?"

Molly looked up and smiled. "I am only looking."

For a snowy day, there were a lot of people in there. Of course, it was payday, so everyone had a little money. Molly started looking for Gary. She didn't see him anywhere. *Oh, well. He will find me.* As she turned around to go to the shoe department, she bumped into this man in uniform. "Oh, I am so sorry. I didn't see you there. It is so crowded in here."

"That's alright, Miss," he said with a real southern accent. Molly couldn't help but notice his dark wavy hair. He smiled as he turned and walked away. Molly couldn't keep from watching him. He was a small man, and his smile was so nice. She had the strange feeling she had seen him before. Maybe she had. *Oh, well. I must look for Gary,* she thought.

Molly was looking at the shoes when she felt someone touch the back of her hair. She turned around to see Gary. "What's going on, you beautiful doll? You want a date?"

"Yes, I do," she said, as she gave him a big hug.

"Boy, you are a easy pick up."

They both laughed.

"Who was the man I saw by you?"

"I don't know. I bumped into him. I felt like I knew him, but I had never seen him before. It was really weird."

"He is a tech sergeant. He has been in a long time. I watched him walk away from you Molly. He stopped and turned around and looked at you for a few seconds. If he was a younger guy, I might have been jealous, but he was too old for you. And, I know you only have eyes for me."

"That's right, honey."

"We better get going before the snow gets any deeper."

"Okay, but I got to pay for the shoes. They are so cute, and they are ankle boots so they will keep my feet warm.

"You are crazy about shoes, Molly."

"Not as crazy as I am about you."

"Keep it up, cutie, and you know what will happen."

They paid for the shoes and headed out the base exchange, hand in hand, so much in love.

Seven

A few more weeks passed, and the snow just kept pil- ing up. Molly had never seen snow like this. She and Lagatha would have coffee together in the morning. It sure helped to pass the time. Lagatha was from the south, so she really hated the long winters.

Molly thanked Lagatha for the coffee and started down the stairs to her apartment. "I am going to go down to Helina's, if it's not too cold to walk."

She bundled up, and began the trek. As she was walking, there was a car going down the street. It had a couple Air Force guys in it. Molly didn't look over at them, but they had rolled the window down. She could hear them talking. She watched the car go down the street.

As she got closer to Helina's house, the same car was in the driveway. *I guess those guys are getting their palms read,* she thought. Molly just kept walking. She wasn't going to go in while they were there, so she walked a couple more blocks to pass the time. She was getting a little cold. There was a park with a small pond and a few swings. There were some moms with their kids, little ones too young for school, who were ice skating. How fun that looked. They had a fire going. Molly walked closer to watch and stand next to the fire. A lady sitting on the bench spoke and said, "Did you bring your skates?"

"No, I don't have any."

"Well, you must not be from Massachusetts?"

"No, Ma'am, I am not. My husband is in the Air Force. My name is Molly Harper."

The lady said, "Nice to meet you, Molly. I am Gerry, short for Geraldine. Those are my two little boys out there; they sure can skate. They are five and six years of age. The six-year-old didn't have school today; their heating system was out, so we had to find something to do to keep them busy. They have been skating since they started walking. Do you skate, Molly?"

"Yes, but at home in Indiana, we skate indoors at a rink. I don't have any skates. Well, you have not lived until you have skated on a pond."

"I would like to try that sometime."

Molly had stood in front of the fire long enough to get warm.

"Do you live around here, Molly?"

"Yes, about a mile down the street."

"That's a long walk on a cold day. I wasn't going to go this far, but my friend had company, so I just kept walking. I didn't know this park was here. I guess I better get going. It was nice to meet you, Gerry. I hope we will meet again."

"We will be here Sunday afternoon. My husband Eddie likes to skate with the boys. Bring your husband."

"I will if he doesn't have to work. I will try and find some ice skates."

"There is a second-hand store over in Indian Orchard. They always have some."

"Okay, thanks. Hope to see you Sunday."

Molly headed down the street to see if Helina was home. Her feet were really getting cold. As she was walking up on the porch, Helina was coming out the door. "Hi, Helina."

"Hi. What are you doing out in the cold weather? You might freeze to death."

"I wanted to come see you. I came by earlier and you had company."

"That was some Air Force guys my mother knows."

"Oh, I thought they were seeing your grandmother."

"No, not this time."

"I found the park up the street. Oh, yes, when you live in this area you do all the winter sports. Otherwise, you would be stuck inside, and that would really be a long winter."

"I met a real nice lady. She has two little boys. They are good skaters. She invited us there Sunday to skate with them. I hope Gary doesn't have to work. Do you skate, Helina?"

"No, I don't have time for fun. I am surprised you came back to my house. I thought my grandmother scared you. What did she say that upset you so much?"

"She said some things that only I know."

"Well, that's what she does, Molly. She is a fortune teller; she knows things about people."

"I don't believe that."

"Then, how do you explain what she said? I don't know; maybe just a good guess. When did your parents get home?"

"My mother got home a couple days ago."

"I have never met your parents. You told me once that they travel with their job. What do they do, Helina?"

"You sure are a nosey girl, Molly. They are with the circus, so most of their time is spent in Florida in the winter months."

"So, why is your mother home now?"

"Well, I guess she wants to be home. My father is a true gypsy; he never stays in one place very long. My mother and I have made a life without him. Their marriage was arranged when they were really young, so I don't think they ever loved each other. My grandmother is the head of our house. My father is a disappointment to her. I am the only child they had. My mother said that my father probably has other children. But who really knows? I can't believe I am telling you all this. I must go. I have somewhere to go."

"I will walk with you, Helina. Are you going to the cemetery?"

"That is none of your business! Molly, you are the nosiest girl I have ever known. And, for the life of me, I don't know why I like you. We are from two different worlds. But I do like you, so come on and walk with me. After all, it is the way home for you."

"You know, Helina, maybe we are not so different."

"Oh, yes, we are, Molly. You are happily married, and my true love is in the cemetery."

"I am so sorry for you…" Molly started to speak, until Helina said, "Please no more. Let's just finish walking."

They came to the entrance of the cemetery. Helina turned to walk in. Molly crossed the street heading to her apartment.

Sunday arrived, and Molly was so excited. Gary had the day off, and they had purchased ice skates at the second-hand store. They dressed in the warmest clothes. "Let's drive up to the park, Molly. It is too cold to walk. And, if I break my leg, you can drive me to the hospital."

"Oh, Gary, don't be silly."

As they drove into the park, they could see the people skating and warming themselves by the fire. As they got closer to the park benches, Molly heard a voice say, "I am so glad you came." It was Gerry, the lady she met the other day.

"Oh, hi! This is my husband, Gary."

"So nice to meet you." Gerry stood up and waved at the man out on the pond. "I want Eddie to meet you two."

"Where are your little boys?"

"Oh, they are out on the ice with my sister. They will be off the ice in a few minutes for some hot cocoa."

Gerry's husband came off the pond. "This is Molly, the girl I told you about, and her husband, Gary. So nice to meet you kids. So, you going to try ice skating?"

Molly was busy putting on her skates. Then, off she went on the ice.

"Come on, Gary. Get out here."

"Molly, you are doing great!"

"Come on!"

Gary headed out to the ice slowly. Molly skated up to him and got a hold of his arm. Just go slow. You will get the hang of it. As they were coming around the pond, Gary said, "This is fun. I think I will try and go by myself once. Okay, but don't get too brave. You don't want to fall."

After a few times around, they decided to get something hot to drink and talk to their new friends.

"How long have you been in Massachusetts?"

"We got here this summer."

"Well, how do you like this part of the country?"

"We really like it. The winters are cold."

"This is nothing. Wait till it really gets cold."

Molly spoke up and said, "It is really different from where we came from. There are so many different kinds of people."

"What do you mean, Molly?"

"Well, you know, like French, Polish, and Irish folks."

"Yes, we are. When a lot of our parents and grandparents came to this country, they settled in New England. We are proud to be Americans, but we love being Polish Americans or French Americans the best. What about you kids? What are you?"

Molly paused for a minute and looked at Gary.

"Well, Eddie, I guess by the time they got down to Indiana and Kentucky, they forgot about the blood lines. I don't think we talk much about that. I heard my mother say she had some Indian blood in her. I just always thought I was American."

Eddie laughed. "I guess that's good enough."

Molly headed back out on the ice for one more time. It was really getting cold. Gerry and the little boys joined her. Gary and Eddie were sitting by the fire. "So, you like the Air Force?"

"Yes, I do. I like my job. I am a mechanic on the B-52's."

"That sounds like a good job. Are you planning on staying in for twenty? I don't know; too early to tell."

"I was in the Navy for several years. I got tired of not having roots and came back home and met Gerry. I had been a bachelor for a long time. We hit it off pretty good, got married, and started a family. Best thing I ever did! You kids should come to dinner some Sunday."

"I am sure Molly would love that."

"Do you all have a phone?"

"Yes, let me give you the number."

About that time, Gerry and the kids and Molly came walking over.

"I guess we better get these boys home. They are cold and tired," Gerry said.

"Me too," Molly said. "I have had so much fun. You forget how cold it is."

Eight

The weeks were going by fast, and the snow was piling up even faster. Gary had gone into work early and would probably have to stay for twenty-four hours because of the bad weather. Molly crawled back into bed after Gary left for work. As she was lying there, she could hear the snow plow going down the street. One thing about living in New England; they know how to take care of their roads. The snow didn't keep too many people home. Molly decided she better get up and get some of her work done. As she was dusting off the table by the window, she saw Helina trying to walk into the cemetery. She watched her fall over in the snow. *That crazy girl! There is no way she can get to his grave,* Molly thought. She headed for the door and ran out on her porch. She yelled as loud as she could. There weren't too many cars on the street, so the noise wasn't bad. "Helina, come over here!"

Helina didn't look her way. She yelled again, then Helina turned around and saw Molly put her hand up in the air and motion for her to come across the street. Helina tried one more time to get through the snow, but it was too deep. She started across the street. As she got closer to Molly, she could see the

51

big smile on Molly's face. "Helina, you are a crazy girl. Did you really think you could get through two feet of snow?"

"I've done it before."

"Come in. You are wet and cold."

She pulled off her boots. They were full of snow.

"You are going to get sick."

"I will not."

"Yes, you will. I will fix us a cup of hot tea."

"Okay, whatever you want."

"Helina, pull off your socks, and I will put them on the radiator. They will dry fast."

"Molly, you are like a little mother hen."

The tea kettle was whistling. Molly went to the kitchen and poured the tea.

"What do you want in it, Helina?"

"Just tea."

"No cream or sugar?"

"No, thanks, I've never heard of putting cream in hot tea."

"That's how we drink it in my family. My daddy drank his like that. My mother is a coffee drinker, but my sister and I like hot tea like our daddy."

"It sounds like you come from a nice family."

"I do. I sure do miss them. My dad writes me every couple weeks. Are you drying out some?"

"I think so."

Helina looked around. "You have a nice place, Molly."

"Thanks."

"Is that picture of your husband?"

"Yep, that's the love of my life."

"How long have you been married?"

"About six months. Gary came home on leave and we got married, then came up here."

"Did you finish high school?"

"Oh, yes. I couldn't get married until I graduated, so I graduated on a Friday and got married on a Saturday. We had a couple days on a honeymoon. Then, we had to report to the base. I think we are still on a honeymoon."

Molly saw the look on Helina's face change. "Oh, I'm sorry, Helina. I didn't mean to make you sad. I am sorry things didn't work out for you."

"It never would have. We came from two different places. His family would have never let us be together. So, everyone lost. They lost their son, and I lost the only man I will ever love."

"Maybe not, Helina. You are very young. There may be someone else in your life."

"Molly, you always look for the bright side of everything."

"There are a lot of guys at the base."

"Yes, but most of them are only looking for temporary friends. My mother has a guy from the base that comes and sees her. He had come to get his palm read a couple months ago. He really took up a friendship with her. He's from somewhere in the South."

"I thought you said your mother and father are married."

"Oh, they are. It's just someone to talk to, she says. But, I think she really likes him. She and my father have not had a life together for years. I am the only thing they have in common, except their jobs with the circus. My father only comes here about once or twice a year. He puts up the big top. My mother worked with her family when she was younger. Her father and two brothers had a trapeze act. I never saw them perform. It was before I was born. Her father fell and broke his shoulder; they kept the act going for a while, but it finally broke up. The marriage was arranged by their families. They worked together after they were married. My mother traveled with my father and their circus for a long time. My grandmother read palms for the circus. I would go to school sometimes if we stayed in one place long enough. One day, when I was about 13, my grandmother didn't like the way things were going with the circus. She got my mother and me and we came to Massachusetts. They put me in school so I could have a better life. It was a hard time. The kids and people around here didn't think much of gypsies. So, we stayed to ourselves. The Air Force guys love to get their fortune told, and my grandmother has no problem taking their money. My mother does a little sewing, so we get by. That one guy from the base will probably hurt my mother. She said he is so nice. I told her he would be transferred out after a period of time. Well, Molly, you seem to have done it again. You make me talk too much. I must go. My tea cup is empty and my socks are dry."

Molly got Helina's coat for her.

"I enjoyed our time together, Helina."

"Me too, Molly."

"Be careful going home." Molly let her out the door and watched her walk down the street. She stopped for a minute to look into the cemetery, but then headed back down the street.

Nine

A few more weeks passed, and it was still cold. It seemed to snow every couple days. Gary had been working a lot at the base. Gerry had called to ask Molly if she and Gary could come over to dinner on Sunday. Molly was so excited to get out of the apartment. Gary was finally going to have a day off. Eddie had given Gary the directions on how to get to their house. Gerry said to be there about 2 p.m.

"There it is," Molly said. "That's the house."

Gary pulled into the driveway. Eddie was waiting at the door.

"You kids come on in."

As they walked into the living room, they could smell the food cooking. It smelled so good. Eddie took them into the kitchen. Gerry was busy getting the dinner ready.

Molly asked, "What can I do to help?"

"Not a thing. Just have a seat, and we will talk while I get this bread in the oven. It won't be too long before it is ready.

Eddie spoke up and said, "Come on, Gary. We'll go in the living room. The kids want you to see their toy airplane. We'll let the girls get dinner on the table."

"You have a nice house, Gerry."

"Thanks, Molly. We built it a couple years ago. All this ground belonged to Eddie's family when his folks died. The children got the property. Eddie's brother lives down on the corner, and his sister lives as you first turn on our road. So, it is a family affair."

"That nice. I really miss my family. But, I love being married and having my own life with Gary."

"You kids are so young and in love."

"Yes, we are."

"Eddie and I didn't get married until we were thirty, so we started our family right away."

"Gary and I want to have two children some day, but not for a long time. He has three more years in the Air Force, and he might stay in it. It is too soon to tell."

Gerry took the hot bread out of the oven. The smell filled the big kitchen. She handed Molly the butter. "Let's put this on the table."

Molly could hardly wait to eat. Gerry called everyone to the table. Everyone took a seat. The boys wanted to sit by Gary and Molly. Gerry said, "Let us pray."

Eddie said, "Make it a short one. I am hungry."

The kids giggled.

Gerry had cooked a Polish dish with sausage, potatoes, cabbage, and some other things that Molly didn't recognize, but everything tasted really good. Molly loved experiencing all this new stuff. They finished their dinner.

"Let me help you with the dishes," Molly said.

"No, we'll do that later. I made a pie for dessert. We will have our coffee and pie and just talk for awhile."

The little boys had gone to their room to play with their toys.

As they ate their pie, Gary said, "This pie is so good. It tastes like one my dad would make."

"Is your dad a baker?"

"Not anymore. He used to work in a bakery when he was young, but he loves to bake. He is a paper hanger by trade."

"He's a good cook too," Molly said. "I have a lot to live up to. I hope to be a good cook some day."

Gary spoke up and said, "I told you, Molly, we will learn to cook together."

As they were finishing their coffee, Molly noticed that it had started to snow again. "When does it stop snowing?" she asked.

"Well, usually it's all gone by the end of April. We do have long winters."

"Yes, we do," Molly said.

Gerry wouldn't let Molly help her with the dishes. "You kids head on home before it gets too bad out there."

"We sure have had a nice time, and the food was so good! Thank you so much!"

"Well, we sure hope you will come back again," Eddie said. "Maybe some Friday night. The kids always have coke and chips. That is their treat."

"We might just do that."

Gerry came out from the kitchen. "Here, take this with you. It will taste good in the morning with your coffee."

It was two pieces of the pie and half a loaf of that wonderful bread with a stick of real butter.

"Oh my, that's real nice of you."

Molly and Gary said goodbye and headed out the door.

As they backed the car out the driveway, the snow started coming down faster. "I don't know if I will ever get used to this weather. I am cold."

"Well, get over here close to me. The car will warm up some. I will warm you up when we get home."

Molly laughed, "You'd better!"

"I guess they sent us home with this food because they probably know we don't make much money. If they knew what we had in our refrigerator right now, they wouldn't believe it. That pie and bread will really taste good in the morning."

"Yes, it will."

As they were driving down the street, they could see the snow plows out doing their jobs. The plows would push the snow off the road, but the wind would just blow it back again. Gary was driving slowly. They were going past Helina's house. Molly could see Helina's mom talking to someone in a car. It was dark, so Molly could not see very well. "I bet that's her friend that Helina talks about."

"What friend?" Gary asked. "Oh, this Air Force guy that came to get his palm read a while back. Helina's mom got to be friends with him."

"I thought she has a husband."

"She does, but I don't think they have a marriage."

"Well, I believe when you are married, you don't have a man friend."

"I don't think it's that kind of friend, Gary."

"Well, Molly, let me tell you: Most single Air Force guys are not just looking for friendship. They are looking for something else."

"Maybe not. Maybe they are just friends."

"Molly, you think everyone is good and kind, but some people are just out for what they can get."

As they parked the car and headed to the apartment, the snow was really falling. The moon peeked through a cloud and made the snow glisten. It was very cold. Molly reached down and got a handful of snow. She made a snowball and threw it at Gary. She fell down as she threw it. Gary fell down on top of her, giving her a kiss and rolling around in the snow laughing. They were laughing so loud one of the neighbors looked out their window.

"Come on, Molly. We better get inside and get out of these wet clothes."

They got up and out of the snow, and went into the apartment. As they got in the apartment, they started getting out of their wet clothes.

"I am so cold," Molly said.

They hung the wet clothes over a chair by the radiator. Molly ran to the bedroom and jumped in bed. Gary was laughing so hard at her. He stood in the bedroom door and just looked at her.

"What are you looking at?"

"I was just thinking how wonderful it is to be married to you, Molly Harper. Now, scoot over, and I will keep you warm."

Molly pulled back the covers and Gary crawled in.

Ten

A *few weeks passed, and spring was just around the cor-*
ner. That's what everyone was saying. It wasn't snowing
as much, and there was still a lot of snow piled up, but it wasn't as
cold, so some of the snow was melting. It sure was a long winter.

Lagatha had come down to have a cup of coffee. She was
having a bad day. Molly could tell that Lagatha had been crying.

"What in the world is wrong?"

"Well, Sam got orders to go to Vietnam. I knew it could happen, but I just hate it."

"How does he feel about it?" Molly asked.

"Well, he said that's his job."

"At least he won't be fighting. He will be working on the
airplanes."

"I know, but war is terrible."

"What will you do, Lagatha?"

"Oh, I will go home to Virginia."

"I will miss you so much, but we will keep in touch."

"I will write you, Molly. You will have to let me know what happens with you and Helina."

Lagatha got up from the table and thanked Molly for the coffee.

"I have to go over to the base. Would you like to ride along?"

"Yes, I would."

"I never have Sam's car, but he rode with Billy to the base this morning. Let me go up and get my purse and lock the apartment. I'll get my coat and meet you at the car."

"Sounds good. See you in a minute."

Molly grabbed her coat and ran a comb through her hair. She couldn't pass a mirror without checking to see if she looked okay.

Molly got to the car before Lagatha. She got in and was putting on her lipstick when Lagatha opened the car door.

"Okay, let's get to the base and do a little shopping."

"Sounds good to me. This is a real treat. I never get to go to the base without Gary. I even got a couple extra dollars my daddy sent me for an emergency." Molly laughed, "There might be something I can't live without."

As they were driving down the street, Lagatha asked, "Molly, have you seen Helina lately?"

"Not for a few days."

As they were passing Helina's house, they saw Helina's grandmother getting the mail. "Wonder why she bothers with the mail if she can tell the future?" Lagatha asked. "She should know what's in them."

Molly just looked at her. Lagatha started laughing. "I don't believe that stuff either, Lagatha, but I have to say she said some things to me that I still can't understand how she knew."

"Oh, Helina's probably told her."

"Oh, no, Lagatha. No one could have known about this."

As they pulled into the gate at the base, the airman checked the sticker on the back of the car, then waved them in. Molly reached in her purse to check her hair in her compact. "You look fine, Molly. You are the most primpy girl I have ever known."

"Well, it never hurts to look good."

They both laughed as they were getting out of the car. "You don't want to look too good. This base is full of single men."

"Oh, I know, but I only have eyes for my Gary. He knows I am crazy in love with him."

"Well, it is for sure you are crazy."

"We better stop laughing and act like two grown women. We wouldn't want to get thrown out of the base exchange."

"Molly, I am going over to look at the China. I want to get some ordered for my mother before we leave the base. The price is so reasonable."

Molly headed over to look at the sweaters. "I will find you when I get through ordering the China."

"Okay, Lagatha."

Molly looked at the sweaters, but saw nothing she really could afford. So, she headed to the perfume counter. Oh, how she loved to smell good. The lady behind the counter said, "May I help you?"

"Yes, I just wanted to smell the one right here."

"This one is our best seller," the lady said.

Molly stuck out her wrist. She gave her a spray. "Oh, that is heavenly."

"Yes, it is," the lady said.

"What is it called?"

"It's called 'Heavenly'!"

"You're kidding?"

"No, that is what it is."

Molly smiled. "Well, they sure gave it a good name. How much is it?"

"Oh, it's on sale today. This two-ounce bottle is $5.99."

"Wow, that's a bargain. I will take it. My husband will love it."

Molly paid the lady and started to look for Lagatha. She kept smelling her wrist. She knew Gary would not mind that she spent the money. She rarely spent any money on herself.

As she looked up, she saw Lagatha coming across the base exchange.

"Are you ready to go?"

"Yes, I got everything ordered. My mother should get the China about the same time I get back to Virginia."

"What did you get?"

Molly stuck out her wrist. Lagatha looked. "No, smell. I got some new perfume."

"Oh, that's heavenly."

"You have smelled it before?"

"No, why do you ask?"

"Well, it is called 'Heavenly.'"

"Oh, that's a great name."

They started to laugh.

"Well, I guess I know what you will be doing tonight!"

Molly just smiled as they headed off the base and down the road.

As they were driving, Molly asked Lagatha, "I know you don't believe in having your palm read, but do you want to stop by Helina's just for fun?"

"No, but if Helina is out we can stop and say hi."

As they turned on the street, Molly could see that someone was in the front yard. It was some Air Force guy talking to Helina.

"Stop, Lagatha."

So she pulled over in front of the house. Molly got out.

"Come on, Lagatha."

"No, I will just wait here."

Helina looked up and said, "What do you want?"

"I just wanted to stop by and see how you are."

Then the side door opened, and Helina's mother walked out with that Air Force guy friend of hers. They were just laughing. "Helina, your grandmother needs you in the house."

Helina headed in the house.

Molly yelled, "I'll see you later."

Helina just waved and hurried in. Molly stood there for a second, then went and got in Lagatha's car.

"What do you think is going on there?"

"I don't know, but that guy with Helina's mother was sure looking at you."

"I guess the guy Helina was talking to is that guy's buddy. I bet they hitchhiked from the base. Helina said they are just friends. He came there a couple times to have his palm read and they just hit it off."

"He is a nice looking guy. He sure is short. He kind of looks like you, Molly. His hair is the same color."

"Lagatha, you are so silly. Maybe he is a gypsy."

"Oh, no. Helina said he is from the South. She said he talks real southern."

"Well, it looks like to me he has something going on with Helina's mother. He was sure looking at you."

"Yes, I saw that, but I know why. I bumped into him at the base exchange once when Gary and I were in there shopping. We exchanged a couple words. Gary said he watched him walk away, then turn around and watch me for a few seconds. I probably look like someone he knows. Well, let's get home. It is getting late."

Eleven

Spring was in the air. The snow piles had melted. The trees were beginning to bud. Spring in New England was beautiful. Molly had gotten a letter from Lilly. She was engaged to the guy she had dated for a couple years. He was away at college. Molly was so happy for her. Danny was a great guy. They would be very happy. Lilly hadn't set the date yet, but Molly knew she probably would not get to go home to be in the wedding. That made her sad, but Lucy and Annie would get to be in it. Lilly said mother and daddy are fine and send their love.

Well, the day had come to say goodbye to Lagatha and Sam. Molly promised to write. Gary told Sam to be safe and maybe they would see each other again someday. Lagatha said, "I will send you my new address. You have to keep me up on the secret life of Helina!"

A few more days passed. Molly sure missed Lagatha. Gary knew Molly was sad. Molly had another bad dream. Gary hated it for her. She would be upset for a couple of days after having the dream.

"Sometimes it makes me so sad," Molly told Gary. "I didn't think I ever wanted to know anything about my real father, but as I've gotten older and think about someday when we have children, I would like to know something about him. What did he look like? Do I look like him? All I know is he was short and had dark wavy hair, and he was killed in a car wreck before I was born. That is not much to know. I am sure my mother knows more. She's just not going to tell it. I feel guilty wanting to know. I have such a wonderful daddy, and he doesn't understand. He is the only father I know. He is such a good father, and I could not love him any more if his blood ran in my veins. And I love my brothers and sisters, and I am so grateful to be in my family. I would not change a thing. But, there is an empty place in my heart I need to fill."

Gary held Molly in his arms. "I am so sorry, Molly. I will do whatever it takes to find some answers for you. When we go back to Indiana, we will go to Kentucky and we will find his grave and some of his family, and maybe find out something about him. We don't have to tell anyone about it."

Molly held on tight to Gary. "You are a wonderful husband. I love you."

A few days later, Billy and Nancy came by to see if they wanted to go see a movie on base. "That sounds great. What time does it start?"

"I think about four o'clock. Let's go now and stop on base at the Burger Basket and get something to eat."

They got in Billy's car and headed for the base. Nancy asked Molly, "Have you heard from Lagatha yet?"

"No, but I will the first chance she gets."

Gary and Billy went up to order the burgers, while Molly and Nancy found a table. Molly heard someone yell, "Hey airman Harper!" As she looked up, some guy was walking toward Gary and Billy. "Hey, Steve! What are you doing?"

"I'm just grabbing something to eat. You know Billy?"

"Yes, nice to see you. Let me get this tray of food and you come over here. I want you to meet Molly. Okay?"

They walked over to the table. Gary put the food down.

"Steve, this is my wife, Molly; and this is Nancy, Billy's wife."

"Nice to meet you, Steve. Gary has said a lot of nice things about you. I hear you didn't care much about our winter, Molly."

"I have never seen so much snow in all my life. Do you like it?"

"Yes, I am from Upstate New York, so I am used to it."

"I am just glad summer is almost here," Molly said. "We are on our way to the movies. Do you want to join us?"

"Oh, no. Thanks, but I don't want to be a fifth wheel."

"So, you are a single guy?"

"Yes, haven't found the right girl yet."

"Be careful, Steve. Don't tell Molly that, or she will be finding you a wife!"

"That might be okay. Let me know, Molly, if you find one," Steve laughed. "Catch you guys later. Nice to meet you, Molly and Nancy."

Molly looked over at Gary. "He sure seems like a nice guy. We should have him over to the apartment sometime."

"We can do that," Gary said.

"How about your next weekend off?"

"I will ask him over for dinner."

"I wonder what he would think of a gypsy girl?"

"Molly, you wouldn't dare."

"Oh, yes I would. It's about time Helina got a life."

The next morning Molly was up early. She had Gary's coffee made before he was out of bed. She was pouring him a cup when she heard him say, "Did the alarm not go off?"

UnOpen Dream

"No, I turned it off. I was coming in to wake you up and give you your coffee. What's the special treatment for?"

"Oh, just cause I love you so much."

"I love you too. What are you going to do today?"

"I am going to get your uniform ironed, then walk down to Helina's."

"Oh, boy. I bet you are cooking up a plan."

"Yes, I am."

"Molly, don't try to play cupid."

"I am not. I am just going to try and direct a few arrows her way. I just want her to be happy. She has had such a sad life, and she is so young."

"But, she has a long life ahead of her, and she will find her own happiness."

Gary finished getting ready for work. He gave Molly a big ol' kiss and headed out the door.

"Good luck today, cupid."

Molly got her ironing done and cleaned herself up. The sun was shining bright, and it was a nice warm morning. Molly loved walking in the morning and smelling the clean fresh air. It made her feel so good and happy. As she got closer to Helina's house, she hoped there would be no one there getting a palm reading.

Molly couldn't keep from thinking again about what Helina's grandmother had said when she read her palm. There was no way she could have known that. It was just a wild guess. "Your father is closer than you think"; those words just stuck in her mind. Her dreams drove her crazy. *If only I could see the man's face,* she thought. *I guess it's Warren.* She felt strange saying his name.

As she got close to Helina's house, she could see Helina and her mother talking on the front porch. Her mother looked like she had been crying. Molly stopped and waited at the end of the

70

sidewalk out next to the street until Helina told her to come in the yard. Helina's mother went in the house, and Helina walked out to Molly. "What are you doing out so early, Molly?"

"I wanted to talk to you."

"I was just getting ready to go to the cemetery, but my mother was upset so I needed to talk to her."

"Is there anything I can do to help?"

"No, her friend is getting transferred to another base, and she doesn't want him to go."

"Well, maybe he will get sent back here again."

"No, he is going to transfer to an Air Force hospital. Then, they will treat him for a few months, and he will get discharged."

"He must be pretty sick if he is getting out. My mother said he has something wrong with his stomach, but he also has his twenty years in. I told my mother not to get too close to him; he would break her heart."

"Is your mother in love with him, Helina?"

"No, she said she just likes him a lot. She said it wasn't a love affair. He is still in love with some woman back where he came from. She had his baby, but he didn't marry her. He said he lived to regret that. He listened to his sister instead of his heart. He only saw his little girl once when she was a baby and a couple times when she was older. He said he saw her at a park once. He wanted badly to go up to her, but he had promised to stay out of their lives."

"Well, that sure is a sad story. I hope your mother will be okay."

"Oh, she will. There will be another Air Force guy come along. Molly, you have a way about you. I don't know why I tell you so much. You want to walk over to the grave site with me?"

"Yes, I do."

As they walked over, Molly watched Helina straighten up the flowers on the grave. Helina kneeled down and kissed the top of the headstone. Molly felt so sad for her. Helina turned around and walked away. Molly reached over and touched Helina's hand.

"I am so sorry this happened to you, Helina. But when are you going to stop punishing yourself? He made the choice to kill himself. Maybe there were some other things going on in his life that you didn't know about. It is time that you start to live. There is a great big world out there. You can choose to embrace it and move forward, or you can let it put you out like smothering a fire on a candle. We all have a purpose in life, and I don't think yours is coming to this cemetery every day. I think God puts people in our path to help us find a new path to travel."

"Oh, Molly, how did you get to know so much for someone as young as you are?"

"I don't have an answer for that, Helina. All I know is you need to be happy."

Helina started walking toward home. "See you soon, Molly."

"Hey, Helina, on Saturday at 6 o'clock, we are having some people over. Please come and meet Gary and spend some time with me. I promise you some good southern cooking, or at least southern Indiana cooking. Please think about it."

Helina just waved as she walked up the street.

Twelve

The weekend rolled around, and it was a nice warm day. Molly and Gary had made some Sloppy Joe's to go on a bun, plus some mac and cheese and brownies. Nancy and Billy were coming and so were Steve, Cliff, and a couple other guys from the base. Molly was sure hoping that Helina would come by, but she really didn't think she would. Molly had the apartment fixed up cute. She had a red and white plastic table cloth on her table in the living room, and had the radio on the favorite station.

Gary stopped stirring the Sloppy Joe in the skillet and came in the living room and took Molly's hand. Can I have this dance? They danced around the room. Molly loved to dance with Gary. They were just about to kiss when Steve said, "Is this a private party?"

"Oh, no, come on in. We were just having fun."

Molly held the screen door open for Steve.

"Here, I got some soda pop. You might want to put it in the fridge."

Gary said, "Molly, turn off the fire on the skillet. We don't want to burn our food."

Nancy and Billy came in the door. "Boy, something smells good. Here, Molly; I baked some beans to go with the rest of the food."

"Great, I love your baked beans, Nancy."

"Who else is coming?" Nancy asked.

"Oh, a couple of guys that work with Gary and Steve. Steve spoke up and said, "Molly, I am surprised you didn't invite a girl for me."

"Well, she did," Gary said. "But, she might not show."

"Who is she?"

Molly glared at Gary.

"Oh, she's Molly's friend that lives up the street."

Martin and Gabby came in the door. "Let's eat. We are starved. We have been looking forward to this food all week. You married guys have it made. You don't have to eat that food at the base."

"The plates are on the cabinet. Everyone help themselves."

Everyone was busy getting food when Molly saw someone coming up the driveway. "That looks like Helina." But she had on a pair of pedal pushers and a blouse with a pair of white tennis shoes. Molly could not believe her eyes. She ran out the door to greet her. "You look beautiful. I am so glad you came. Your dress is so different."

"Well, if I am going to start a new life, I better dress the part."

Molly grabbed her hand. "Come on in."

As they walked in the door, Molly said, "Hey, everyone, this is my good friend, Helina."

Gary walked over and said, "So glad to meet you. Molly talks about you all the time."

"I bet she does."

Gary laughed. "I'm sure you know, Molly is never at a loss for words."

"Let's get some food, Helina."

"Oh, I'll try some of your cooking. It does smell good."

Helina filled her plate with a little of everything. I do want one of those chocolate brownies. Gary was busy talking to Martin and Billy. Nancy was talking to Gabby about some Italian place in Massachusetts. He was from Boston, and he was Italian. He joined the Air Force to see the world, and ended up back in Massachusetts at Westover AFB. He said he would have to re-enlist to get to see anyplace else.

Molly and Helina had gone out on the porch to eat their food. "What do you think, Helina? Do you like the food?"

"It tastes good. I've never had this Sloppy Joe before. It is sloppy."

Steve came out on the porch. "Do you mind if I join you?"

"Oh, no, that's fine."

Molly could tell Helina got a little nervous. Steve told Molly he sure enjoyed the home cooking. I miss my mom's cooking. I try to go home whenever I get a long weekend."

"You are from Upstate New York?"

"Well, I am really from Rochester, New York. Where are you from, Helina?"

"Oh, I am from everywhere. My family used to travel a lot. I've been here several years."

"What do you do for fun, Helina?"

"I haven't been much into fun lately. I help my mother and grandmother. I am thinking about getting some kind of job."

"What kind of work would you like to do?"

"Oh, I don't know. I am used to hard work, so anything would be all right. I saw a sign in the dry cleaner store, the one right outside the gate at the base that said, 'Help Wanted.' I might check that out."

Gary had walked out on the porch to see what was going on. He had turned up the radio. You could hear Dean Martin singing, "Everybody Loves Somebody Sometime." That was one of Molly and Gary's favorite songs. Gary reached out for Molly and turned her around a couple times and then pulled her close to him. "You want to dance?"

"Not now, you silly thing."

Steve said, "You two are sure crazy about each other."

Helina jumped up and said, "I must go Molly. I had a nice time."

"Oh, don't go yet," Steve said. "I would like to get to know you."

"Maybe another time. It was nice to meet you."

Helina started off the porch. "Molly, I will see you soon. Thanks. Goodbye."

Helina crossed the street and started walking toward the cemetery. Molly was praying to herself, *Please don't let her go in there. Let her go on down the street to her house.*

Molly watched, and Helina went on down the street. Molly knew then that Helina had taken that first step in going on with her life.

Thirteen

*A few days later, Molly was busy in the apartment dust-*ing and sweeping. She heard someone knock on the door. The door was open, but the screen door was locked. It had finally gotten warm enough to have the door open in the mornings. Molly yelled, "Just a minute."

"It's me, Molly."

That sounds like Helina! Molly hurried to the door. "Hi! Come on in. What a nice surprise. Well, I was going to the cemetery, but I changed my mind and came to see you."

"Okay, Helina, that's a good thing. You want a cup of coffee?"

"Sure, that would be nice."

"What have you been doing?"

"Well, I went to the cleaners by the base and applied for the job, and they hired me!"

"That's great!"

"I start on Monday."

"That's only four days away."

"I know. I am kind of nervous. I know I can do the work. I am just not used to being around a lot of people."

"What did your mother say?"

"Oh, not much. She's still sad over her friend getting orders to go to Texas. She thinks she will hear from him or see him again someday. She's fooling herself."

"Speaking of guys, Helina, what did you think of Steve?"

"He seemed real nice."

"Would you like to see him again?"

"Maybe I would."

"Great, what about this weekend?"

"How do you know he wants to see me again?"

"Oh, I just know he does. I will talk to Gary tonight when he comes home, and we will get it fixed up. We'll go on a double date."

"Molly, I don't have a lot of nice clothes like you wear."

"Don't worry, I have enough. We are about the same size. You can wear something of mine. You are so kind. No, Helina, that's what friends do. And, you and I are good friends!"

Saturday rolled around. Gary and Steve had made plans for their double date. Steve was more than happy to take Helina out. Steve had said there was a great little fish and chips restaurant on the ocean, about 30 miles away. The drive would be nice, and Molly was dying to see the ocean. Steve wanted to pick up Helina at her house, but she said not this time. She preferred to meet him at Molly's.

Helina got there early so Molly could tell her if she looked okay. "Helina, you look great."

"Thank you, but this is the same outfit I wore when I met Steve."

"He will not notice anything, except how pretty you are. Here, put a little bit of this lipstick on, and put a little of my new perfume behind your ear."

"I'll put the lipstick on, but I will pass with the perfume. You have enough on for the both of us."

Molly looked at her and smiled. "Gary says I always get carried away with my perfume."

"You sure are a primpy girl."

Gary walked in. He had been in the bedroom getting ready. "Oh, hi, Helina. You ready for your date?"

"I guess."

"Don't worry, Steve is a great guy. We will have a lot of fun."

Steve walked up on the porch.

"Come on in. We are just about ready to go."

Steve walked over to Helina. "It is so nice to see you."

Helina just smiled.

As they drove up in front of the restaurant, Molly asked, "Is this it?"

"Yes, it is," Steve said. "It's called the Clam Shack. They have great seafood. It looks like a shack, but wait till you taste the fish and fried clams! You can't live in New England without trying the seafood."

They ordered their food from a window. They had the fish and chips wrapped in newspaper. That was so odd, Molly thought. But, so was eating fried clams. She really didn't know much about clams, but they sure tasted good.

When they finished their food, Steve said, "Grab the cooler and the blanket. Let's get down to the beach. We just go across the road and walk just a bit, and we will be there. Molly grabbed Gary's hand. "I am so excited."

"Molly slow down; we have all day. The ocean is not going anywhere."

Helina started to laugh,

"She is the silliest girl I've ever known."

As soon as they got to the sand, Molly kicked off her shoes and started running to the ocean. "Come on, Gary! Let's get our feet wet!" When Molly's feet hit the water, the waves splashed against her legs. She screamed, "It's so cold! But I love it!"

As they were playing around in the water, Molly could see Steve and Helina sitting on the blanket talking. "I am so glad you came today, Helina. I really do like spending time with you. It's been a long time since I've been on a date."

"I find that hard to believe, Steve. You are such a nice guy. I am sure there are lots of girls around the Air Force base that would enjoy your company."

"I was engaged, Helina, before I joined the Air Force, but there was a terrible accident. I told my girlfriend I was planning on joining the Air Force before we got married and that I wanted to stay in for twenty years and retire with a nice pension. She didn't like that idea. She wanted me to work in my dad's hardware store. I had enough of that. I wanted something more. She left my house that night in her car. It was raining and cold. She lost control of the car, hit a tree, and was killed. I have always felt like it was my fault. It just broke my heart. It has been a few years. You are the first girl I have wanted to spend time with. Molly told me you had your heart broken too."

"Yes I did. I didn't think I would ever be able to go on with my life. But Molly has really helped me see that I have to."

Steve reached down and put his hand on hers. Helina put her head on Steve's shoulder, as she watched the waves come into the shore.

Fourteen

As the weeks passed, Steve and Helina began spending a lot of time together. Summer was going way too fast. Molly had been dreaming a lot. She hated that dream; it took her so far then stopped. She knew by now that man had to be Warren. She didn't understand how she could have this connection to a man she didn't know, a man that she had never seen a picture of, a man that was her real father but had died before she was born. But it was like he was calling to her. Maybe her mother hadn't told her the whole story? Then, she didn't understand how Helina's grandmother could have told her those things. Some days, she just couldn't get it out of her head.

As summer was slipping away, Molly had been busy helping Nancy pack to go home. Billy's time was up, and he and Nancy were going back home. Molly was sure going to miss them, but she knew they would always be friends.

Molly had not seen a lot of Helina since she took that job at the cleaners, but Gary said that Steve had taken her out a few times and they really liked spending time together. Molly just knew they were right for each other.

Molly was busy in the kitchen when she heard a knock on the door. She went to the door, but didn't see anyone. She started to walk away when her brother Larry jumped out and said, "Surprise!"

Molly yelled, "Larry, what are you doing here?"

"We came to see you!"

"Oh, I am so glad to see you! Where is Sharyl?"

"She is in the car."

Sharyl came walking around the apartment house. "It's so great to see you in person."

"Did you get my letter?"

"Yes, but I didn't think you would get out so soon."

"Well, the Marines gave us a two-month early out, so we decided to drive up here form South Carolina before we go to Indiana, and then to California."

"Gary will be so glad to see you. Get your suitcase, and come on in!"

"Your apartment is so nice."

"Thanks! It's small, but we don't need much room. Let me show you where the bathroom is. Just make yourself at home. I will make a pot of coffee, and we will just talk until Gary gets home. Then I will cook supper. I have a chicken in the freezer I bought payday, just for when you all got here."

"Fried chicken. That sounds good!"

The afternoon went by fast as they were finishing their coffee. Molly saw Gary pull in the driveway. "He is going to be so surprised to see you two!"

Gary walked in with a smile on his face. He shook Larry's hand and gave Sharyl a hug. "It is so nice to meet you, Sharyl. It is so nice of you to drive up here to see us. So they let you guys out early?"

"Yes, a couple of months early. I am glad to have my four years over."

"Molly says she is frying chicken for us tonight. That will make the trip worthwhile. Let me get out of this uniform and we will get caught up."

Molly headed for the kitchen. "I better get this chicken ready to fry. Do mashed potatoes sound good to you all?"

"Sounds great. We haven't had much home cooking. What can I do to help, Molly?"

"Oh, you just sit there and relax while we talk."

Gary came out of the bedroom in his jeans and said, "Come on, Larry. Take a ride with me. I need to go down to the store and pick up some Cokes. We usually have Kool-Aid, but this is a special occasion. Do you need anything, Molly?"

"Get something sweet to go with coffee."

"Okay. Be back in a few."

As Gary was driving down the street, he saw the old man on the corner with his vegetable and fruit cart. He was dressed in old torn clothes, but was fairly clean. Gary always liked to talk to him, and he always gave him a few extra vegetables in his paper bag. He pulled over to stop and say hi. "How are you today, Mr. Snapp?"

"I am well. Thank you."

"Got fruit that you need to sell today at a fair price?"

"Yes, I do. How about a few peaches? You need to eat them today."

"Okay, we will."

"How much do I owe you?"

"Nothing today."

"Thank you, Mr. Snapp."

"No need to thank me. How is your wife, Otela?"

"She is doing well. She is on the other side of town. She is selling melons today."

"Well, I better go. My brother-in-law is in the car. We are on our way to get some Cokes. See you soon!"

"Does he live close by?" Larry asked. "I don't think so. He pushes that cart all over this town. I guess his wife does the same. He seems like a happy old man."

As they pulled up in front of the little grocery store, Gary parked the car, and Larry followed him in. The man behind the counter spoke to Gary. "How are you today?"

"I am fine. Thank you. This is my brother-in-law, Larry. He and his wife just got out of the Marines, so they came to see us and your nice state of Massachusetts."

"Nice to meet you. Haberjack is my name."

He reached out to shake his hand. "I am an old leatherneck myself. So, where you headed when you leave here? I am going to see my family in Indiana, then on to California. That's where my wife is from."

"I spent a few days there when I was being shipped out. Pretty place. But they kept saying some day it was going to fall in the ocean."

Gary paid for the Cokes and cookies.

"Nice to meet you, Mr. Haberjack."

"Same here, Larry. Have a safe trip."

As they were walking out to the car, Larry said, "He sure seems like a nice guy."

"He is. The people here in New England are hard to get to know: but once they know you, they are really nice."

Gary could smell the fried chicken as they walked up on the front porch. Molly had the table set. Gary handed Sharyl the Cokes. "You can fill the glasses."

"That sounds good to me."

"I can hardly wait to have some of the fried chicken," Larry said. "Sharyl has not mastered the kitchen yet."

"Well, I am just learning, so I hope it is good."

As they were eating, Molly couldn't help but notice the chicken was still a little bloody on the one side. "I am so sorry! I don't think I fried it long enough."

"It's great," Larry said. "I like rare chicken."

They all got a big laugh out of it. Molly got up from the table to go make a pot of coffee. "We can drink our coffee out on the porch. We have to enjoy the last days of summer. Winter comes really early here. You two will be in sunny California this winter. So that's where you will make your home, Larry?"

"Yes, Sharyl's family is there. I hope Dad and Sara will be able to come see us sometime."

"Oh, I am sure they will."

A couple days had passed and it was time to say goodbye to Larry and Sharyl. Molly hated goodbyes; she always cried. Larry had the car packed, and Sharyl had the route mapped out, so they hugged and kissed goodbye.

"Tell everyone in Indiana we said hi."

Molly told Sharyl to be sure and send their new address when they got settled. Molly cried as she watched them drive away. Gary pulled Molly close to him and held her for a few minutes. "Don't cry, sweetheart. Just think, the next time you see them, you will be able to fry chicken and get it done."

"Oh, Gary!"

They both started to laugh.

Fifteen

A *few days had passed since Larry and Sharyl had left.* Summer was coming to an end. It didn't last as long in Massachusetts as it did back home in Indiana. Fall would come soon. It was beautiful in New England in the fall, but winter was long and cold.

Molly was busy sweeping the porch when she saw Helina coming down the sidewalk. She was so glad to see her.

"Hi, Helina!"

"Oh, it is so good to see you. I have missed you!"

"I have been busy working. I really like my job at the cleaners. But I have the day off, and I wanted to come and see you—and to tell you I am going home with Steve to meet his parents."

"Oh, that's so great! I know you two will get married."

"I really care about him, Molly. I just want to thank you for not letting me just curl up and die; for showing me that there is more life to live."

"What does your mother think?"

"She doesn't say much; whatever makes me happy. She is still missing that airman. She did get a postcard from him; he was in Texas in the hospital with stomach trouble. He is supposed to get discharged and then go home to Kentucky. She liked him a whole lot more than he liked her. I think he just wanted to be friends. But I am sure she will find another Air Force guy. She seems to have a history of that. They come to get their palms read, and she finds one that she likes. I don't think she would miss me at all if I left. I sure hope his parents like me."

"Oh, Helina, they will just love you. I liked you the first time we met, even if you didn't want to be friends."

"Thank goodness you wouldn't leave me alone. You forced me to come out of my shell. Now I have Steve in my life, and I am happy again."

"When will you be leaving to go meet his parents?"

"We will leave Saturday morning. We'll come back late on Sunday."

"Be sure and come down Monday after you get off from work and tell me all about it. I will be so anxious to hear how things went."

"Well, I'd better get back to the house. My grandmother has a group of new airmen coming in to get their fortunes told. She wants me to help her get the room ready. She sure can convince them she knows what she is doing. They want to know if they will get shipped out to Vietnam or if they will meet a girl. She loves taking their money. I'll see you when I get back, Molly."

"Have a good time, Helina."

Molly watched Helina walk back down the street. She never once looked over into the cemetery. Molly knew Helina would never forget her first love, but she knew this love for Steve would grow into something wonderful.

Molly finished sweeping the porch. The wind had picked up, and the leaves were blowing. The leaves were beginning to get a little color. Fall was so beautiful there, but it didn't last long.

Molly went into the house to make some cookies for Gary. He loved sugar cookies, and she usually had everything she needed. She checked all the ingredients. She had everything, but was a little short on vanilla. Regardless, she figured she could make it work. Molly put the cookie dough in the oven and went over to sit down until the timer went off.

Molly had been dreaming a lot again lately—the same dream, except this time the airman that she bumped into at the post exchange was in her dream. He was a lot like the man in her original dream. Why this dream would not stop was such a puzzle to her.

It's like it is trying to tell me something, she thought. Maybe it is my real father trying to talk to me from the grave. Oh that's silly! I know that can't happen.

Molly could hardly wait until Gary got home from work; she needed to talk to him about her dream. He always made her feel better. Molly went in the kitchen to check the cookies, just as the timer went off. The whole apartment smelled like cookies. She took them out of the oven; they looked good! They would sure taste good after supper with a cup of coffee. Molly placed the cookies on the counter to cool. She went back in the living room to rest a few minutes. She soon fell asleep. As she was sleeping, the dream came back:

The man was pushing the same little girl on the swing, but she wasn't little anymore. It was a bigger girl. The girl was laughing. She jumped down out of the swing and started running toward the man that was pushing her. But when she looked up, he was gone. She started yelling, "Where are you?"

And she woke herself up. She sat up on the couch with her heart pounding as if she had been running. *Why can't I see that man's face? It has to be Warren I am dreaming about,* she thought, *but why?* She couldn't keep from thinking about what Helina's grandmother had said to her, and about the fact that the airman in the post exchange seemed like he knew her, and how she felt something strange when she talked to him. She thought for a minute. Maybe he was Warren. He was a small man with dark hair.

Oh my, Molly, she thought to herself. *Stop! I must be losing my mind. Warren is dead. He was killed in a car wreck before I was born. I have got to stop thinking about him.*

She heard Gary come in the front door.

"I smell cookies! Where is my sweet wife?"

Molly ran into his arms. "I love you, Gary."

"I love you too, Molly."

"Please hold me," Molly said, as she started to cry.

"What is wrong, honey?"

"I can't get that dream out of my head."

"It's okay, Molly. I promise you when we go to Indiana on leave in the spring, I will take you to Kentucky and we will find Warren's grave and find out something about him. Your mother and daddy won't have to know anything about it."

Molly wiped her tears. "I don't want to hurt my daddy. I love him so much. He has been a wonderful father to me, but sometimes you just need to know some things."

Gary pulled Molly up in his arms, her feet off the floor.

"I promise you, Molly. We will get that dream out of your head."

Sixteen

A few days passed. Molly was hoping to see Helina.

If she doesn't come down today, Molly thought, I will go to her house when she gets off work. I just know Steve's parents will like her.

Molly went out on the porch to check the mail. The wind was blowing. It would soon snow; they always had snow for Christmas. It would be sad this year. Nancy and Billy had gone home; Molly missed them a lot. Molly went back into the house. She wanted to address her Christmas cards; she couldn't believe Christmas was right around the corner. She turned on the radio to hear some Christmas music. The weatherman was talking about a winter snow storm that could be coming their way.

There was a knock on the door. Molly jumped! It scared her for a moment. Who could that be? As she opened the door, there stood Helina.

"Come in! I am so glad to see you."

Helina was smiling so big. She gave Molly a hug.

"Something big has happened," Molly said. "You have never given me a hug before."

Helina started laughing. "Molly you are so silly. Nothing big has happened; just something wonderful."

She held out her hand. There was a ring on her finger.

"Oh, you got engaged?"

"Yes, and married the same day!"

"What?!" Molly screamed. "I guess his parents really liked you?"

"Yes, they did. I don't know what happened. We knew we loved each other. We just got married. I have never been so happy. I never thought I would feel like this, but Steve is a wonderful guy. I know we will have a wonderful life together; and I owe it all to you, Molly. You made me see that life is so worth living. Thank you so much. You are the best friend in the world."

"What did your mother say?"

"She was happy for me. I think she will be glad to get rid of me. But my grandmother wasn't too happy. She knows I will go with Steve when he gets transferred. She will miss me. I always felt closer to her than my mother."

"Are you and Steve going to get a place together?" Molly asked.

"Yes, we are going tomorrow to look for an apartment. I am so excited to have a home with Steve and start a life together."

"We will all go out and celebrate. You can't get married without a party."

"That sounds good to me. I've got to get going. I will talk to you this weekend. Thanks again, Molly. I will never be able to thank you enough."

Seventeen

*M*ore *weeks passed, and now Christmas was only a week* away. Molly couldn't wait for Gary to get home tonight. They were going to get their Christmas tree. There was a Christmas tree lot down in town. So they were going to bundle up and go get one. It had to be small, because the apartment was small. But Molly knew it would be beautiful. Gary loved Christmas as much as she did. They didn't have a lot of decorations, but enough to make it look good. Molly had so many wonderful memories surrounding Christmas when she was a child. They always had a big tree. Jack would always put the angel on the top. They had a village under the tree with a train that went around. Larry, Molly, Lilly, Lucy and Annie would all lie on the living room floor and watch the train go around, and they would pretend they lived in that village. Christmas was a wonderful time at the Preston home, with lots of good food. Sara and Richard loved to bake and make candy for the family.

Molly heard Gary coming in the door. She ran to give him a kiss and jumped up in his arms.

"You are sure in a good mood, Molly!"

"I know. We are going to get our tree."

"Let me go get out of this uniform and put on some warm clothes. It looks like you are ready. I am, and my daddy sent us $10 in our Christmas card, so we can stop and get a burger on the way."

"That sounds great."

As they were driving to the tree lot, Molly said, "I am so happy Helina and Steve got married."

"Me too," Gary said. "Steve is so much in love with her; almost as much as I love you, baby doll."

"Oh, Gary, we sure are happy. I love you too. Oh, there is a place to park. Pull in. I want to go find my tree."

"Hold on, Molly. Don't jump out of the car yet."

Gary turned off the engine, and Molly was out of the car. It was so cold, but it didn't seem to slow Molly down.

"Hey, Gary. Over here!"

"Where are you, Molly?"

Over here by the trees."

Gary laughed. "Which one, Molly?"

As he turned around, Molly poked her head out.

"I found our tree. Look! It's perfect!"

"That's a nice one, Molly, and the price looks right. Let's go pay the man and get it on the car."

As they were putting the tree on top of the car, they heard someone yell, "Hey kids!"

They looked around to see Gerry and Eddie and their two boys.

"Hi! It's so nice to see you. Merry Christmas!"

"It looks like you found your tree."

"We sure did. Molly loves to pick out her tree."

"At home we would go cut one down, but this is nice. It's too cold to go to the tree farm up here."

"You all looking for a tree?"

"No, we have our tree," Eddie said. "We just needed to get some greenery for the mantel over the fireplace. Gerry likes the mantel to look good for Santa when he comes down the chimney."

Gerry came walking up with the greenery.

"How about going over to the café and having some hot cocoa with us?"

"That sounds great."

"The boys are so excited about Christmas," Gerry said.

"I know what you mean," Gary said. "Molly is like a little kid. She loves Christmas."

"I guess it is hard begin away from your family this time of the year?"

"Yes, it is," Molly said. "But we have made friends, and that makes it nice."

"Speaking of friends, how about you two come over for Christmas dinner?"

"Oh, that sounds nice, but we couldn't interfere with your family."

"Everyone would love to have you. Isn't that what Christmas is all about? We will have dinner about five o'clock. The boys should be calmed down by then."

Molly finished her hot cocoa.

"We better get going, Gary. I want to get my tree up tonight. We will see you all Christmas about five. What can I bring?"

"Just yourself. See you then."

Molly looked at Gary as they were going to the car. "What nice people. We will have to take the little boys a gift."

"We can do that."

"This makes everything so much better; a real Christmas away from home."

Eighteen

A few weeks had passed. Christmas had come and gone; and a new year had arrived. Steve and Helina had gotten settled in their apartment. Molly missed seeing Helina; their apartment was too far away to walk. But they always got together on the weekends if the guys didn't have to work at the base.

Molly was doing her laundry in the basement when she heard Gary calling her name. She went over to the door that led up to their apartment.

"I am down here."

She heard Gary coming down the stairs.

"Hi, honey. What are you doing home so early?"

"They let us off, so here I am. I got my paper for our leave. We get to go home in April for two weeks."

"Oh, Gary, I am so happy. That's only a couple months away."

"Let's go celebrate. I told Steve we would come by and pick them up, and we would go to the airman club on base and have dinner."

"Can we afford that?"

"Yes, I have been putting a little money back each payday."

"Oh, this is great. Let me get these clothes out of the dryer, then I will get upstairs and make myself look pretty for you."

"Molly, you always look pretty to me."

That night at dinner, Molly said, "I am so happy to be with you guys tonight. Gary got his leave. We get to go home for a couple weeks. It will be so nice to see my family."

"Well, we have a surprise too."

"What is it Helina? Tell us."

Steve spoke up and said, "I am being transferred to Anderson Air Force Base on Guam."

"Oh no!" Molly started to cry.

"Don't cry, Molly. I will get to go with him. It could have been Vietnam."

"When do you go?"

"Not till April."

"That is when I go on leave to Indiana," Gary said. "I sure am going to miss you, Steve."

"You probably will be going before too long. They need a lot of mechanics for these B52 bombers. Maybe we will all end up in Guam. That would be fun."

"Where is Guam, anyway? I have never heard of it. How long is the tour, Steve?"

"It is for two years."

Molly asked again, "Where is it?"

It is an island in the Pacific Ocean. It's a long way."

"Don't worry, Molly," Helina said. "We will write to each other."

"I hope we get to tell you goodbye before we go on leave. We will be leaving on the 10th of April."

"That will work out. We are not going to Indiana until the 15th, so we can say goodbye."

"Molly, will you and Gary stay the whole two weeks in Indiana?"

"Yes, except we are going to go to Kentucky for the day to see if we can find my real father's grave."

"Oh, I didn't know anything about that."

"I was going to tell you, Helina, but the time has never been right. My real father was killed before I was born. He left my mother when she was pregnant, and then she was told he was killed in a car wreck. I don't know much about him, except he had dark wavy hair and was short. I never thought much about him, except for these dreams I started to have a few months ago. They upset me so much—and then your grandmother saying what she said to me: 'Your father is not your father' and 'your dream will not open' and 'your father is closer than you think.' It's like he is trying to talk to me from the grave. I know that sounds so silly; but, to have some peace of mind, Gary is going to help me find his grave and maybe some of his family. I don't want my mother or daddy to know about it. I would not hurt my daddy for anything in the world; but there are some things in life you just need to know. I may not be able to find out anything."

"Do you think your mother has told you the whole story?"

"I don't know, Helina. She was so young. I am sure she doesn't want anyone to know, not even my father. I have his name and the town he is from, so we should be able to find out something."

Spring was in the air, and Helina and Molly spent as much time together as they could. Molly told Helina, "I am afraid we will probably never see each other again."

"Oh, yes we will," Helina said. "And we will write. And you will let me know what you find out about your real father."

"Oh, I will! I may not find out anything. They may not want to know me. If I find his grave, I think that will be enough. If he didn't want me in his life, I am sure his family probably won't want anything to do with me either. But we will see what happens."

Time flew by, and it was time to say goodbye to Steve and Helina. One thing about the Air Force; you are always telling someone goodbye. Molly gave Helina a big hug. "We will write every week."

Steve shook Gary's hand. "I will be looking for you two in Guam in about six months."

"I hope not," Gary said.

"We better get going before the tears get too heavy," Molly said, as she was getting in the car.

Helina ran up to the window and said, "Thanks again, Molly. I will never forget you!"

Gary pulled away as Molly was yelling out the window, "Write as soon as you can!"

Nineteen

*T*he day had finally come for the trip back to Indiana. The weather was nice for the long drive home. Gary put the suitcase in the trunk. Molly packed them a cooler so they would have something to eat on the way. As they headed out of town, Gary said, "Molly, what would you think if we went to Kentucky first and looked for Warren's grave and his family?"

"That would be just fine, and then no one would ever know we were down there."

"Okay, sit back and take it easy. We got a long ride ahead of us."

As the sun was setting, Gary asked, "Do you want to stop for a while and stretch your legs, Molly?"

"Yes, let's do that."

"How about getting some supper?"

"Let's get something hot to eat, since we are going to drive the rest of the way."

"Okay, be on the lookout for a place to eat."

A few miles down the road, Molly saw a place that looked nice.

"Let's go there," Molly said. So Gary pulled in.

"It feels great to get out and walk. I hope the food is good. I am hungry."

Molly took Gary's hand. "Let's sit over here. By the way honey, where are we?"

"We are in Ohio. After we eat and get back on the road, if you go to sleep, when you wake up we should be almost to Kentucky."

"But I want to talk to you and keep you company."

"Okay, whatever you want."

They finished their meal and paid the waitress.

"I am going to fill up the gas tank while we are here."

"Okay, Gary. I am going to the ladies room. I will meet you at the car."

Gary was waiting in the car. "What took you so long, Molly? Oh, never mind. I see. You have your hair combed, fresh lipstick on, and you smell really good. All of that to go to sleep."

"I am not going to sleep. I am going to stay awake and talk to you."

Gary leaned over and gave Molly a kiss. "We'll see how long you stay awake."

As they were driving down the road, Gary looked over at Molly. "You getting tired?"

"No, I am just fine. Look at that beautiful moon and all those stars. It sure is a beautiful night."

"Well, my beautiful wife, go to sleep. We have detective work to do tomorrow."

"Okay, I will close my eyes, just to rest for a few minutes.

Molly opened her eyes to see the sun shining through the windshield. "Where are we?"

"We are in Kentucky. I think this is the town the cemetery is located where Warren is buried. Let's go in that little grocery store and get something to drink. Maybe they have coffee."

When they walked in, Molly said, "I smell coffee."

The man behind the counter said, "It is fresh. Help yourself."

"Thanks."

Molly poured her and Gary a cup.

"Do you know if there is a cemetery here?"

"Yes, that is the Parksville Cemetery located down the road by the railroad tracks. You kids looking for someone?"

"Yes. Do you know a woman named Mrs. Evans?"

"Oh, you mean Miss Florence? She lives two miles down the road, before you get to the cemetery on the right, in the concrete block house next to the gas station."

"Thanks," Gary said, and handed the man a dollar for the coffee as they walked out the door. "Let's go find the cemetery."

As they drove down the road, they saw the sign and drove up the drive. "How are we ever going to find his grave?"

"It doesn't look too big. We will just walk it."

Gary stopped the car, and they got out.

"Molly, you take the right side and I will go left. If you find it, just yell for me. I will do the same."

About twenty minutes had passed, and Molly had covered the whole right side of the cemetery. There was a big tree beside a fence, and she felt like she needed to go over where a couple of stones were on the ground. She started to read one. It read, "Sgt. Warren L. Evans."

She stopped. She couldn't believe what she was reading.

Gary heard her call, "I found it!"

He started running over to her.

"Here it is!"

She finished reading. "It says he died February 15, but it didn't say 1946. It was this year," she said, pointing to the recent date on the marker. "I can't believe what I am seeing, Gary! He just died. He has been alive all these years. I just missed seeing him alive by two months. Do you think my mother knew he was alive all this time?"

"I don't know. Let's go see your grandmother."

"Okay, but what if she doesn't believe me? Maybe she doesn't know he had a child."

"Well, if she doesn't want anything to do with us, we'll just leave. I will go to the door and ask her if she knows a Molly Preston, and see what she does."

Gary pulled into the driveway. "I am so nervous!" Molly said. Gary held Molly's hand. "It will be okay, Molly. We need to do this."

Gary got out of the car and walked up to the door. Molly watched him knock on the door. An older lady came to the door. She heard Gary ask her, "Are you Mrs. Evans?" She said, "Yes, I am."

"Do you know anyone by the name of Molly?"

"Oh, dear Lord! I knew she would come. She is my granddaughter!" Gary motioned for Molly to get out of the car. As she walked to the door, she saw the tears on this woman's face. She was holding her hand out to her. "Please come in and have a seat."

"I knew you would come. Molly, when did your mother tell you Warren had died?"

"Well, she told me he died in 1946, before I was born."

"She didn't tell you I called in February when he died?"

"No, but she did tell me where he was buried, in Parksville, Kentucky. We are on our way home on leave and I needed to try and find out something about him. I didn't know if you all wanted anything to do with me."

"Your mother had told Warren the best thing he could do for her was to stay out of her life; she had married and started a new life. And Warren did what she asked. He knew you had a wonderful father, and he didn't want to cause any problems."

"I do have a wonderful father, and it would really hurt him if he knew that I was here. But I just need to know some things about Warren, and it is nice to meet my grandmother."

She started to cry.

"I am so sorry you didn't get to know Warren. He was a nice person, and he regretted what he did to your mother. He lived with a broken heart. He did see you a couple times when you were little. He and Tommy, his cousin, would go up to Indiana to see if he could see you out somewhere. I think he told me he saw you swinging in the park. He would always keep his distance. He did tell me one time he walked by the swing that you were on and gave you a swing from the back and kept on walking. You were about 10 years old. He said by the time you looked around his back was to you and you said thanks, but you couldn't see his face. He told me for years he held on to that little voice that said, "Thank you." I have to tell you, the hardest thing he ever did was to honor your mother's wishes and stay out of your life. I know sometimes he drank too much to kill the pain and guilt. But I know God forgave him. He had a hard time forgiving himself. I am so glad you came, Molly. I am an old woman, and at least now I have met my granddaughter."

"I am happy to meet you, too. I don't want anything from you except to know you and to know about my real father."

"I will tell you whatever you want to know."

"Do you have a picture of him? I would like to know what he looked like."

"Yes, I do."

She got up and went into the other room. Gary looked over at Molly. "You okay?"

"Yes, honey, I am all right. But I think she is in shock that we are here. She said she knew I would come."

A few minutes had passed and Molly heard her grandmother call to her, "Come in here, Molly. I want to show you something."

Molly got up and walked over to the bedroom. Her grandmother was standing there in front of the dresser looking at some pictures.

"This is your real father. This was taken a few months before he died."

Molly gasped for a minute. "This is Warren? It can't be!"

"Yes, it is, Molly. You look a lot like him."

Molly yelled for Gary to come in the room. She was crying.

"What's wrong, honey?"

"Look at this picture."

Gary looked at it and said, "Oh, my Lord. That looks like the man from the post exchange. It can't be."

"You mean I was that close to him and didn't know it? Remember what Helina's grandmother said?"

"I know, Molly. But that stuff is not for real."

Mrs. Evans had a strange look on her face. "Are you saying, Molly, that you saw Warren somewhere?"

"Yes, at Westover Air Force Base, where we are stationed. We live off the base. But I know that was the airman I bumped into. Was he ever at Westover Air Force Base?"

"Yes, he was there a few months ago, before he went to Texas to the hospital and was discharged. He wanted to re-enlist, but his health wasn't good enough. He had such stomach trouble. He only lived a few months after he came home. Here, Molly. This is for you. He said if you ever came, to give you this letter."

Molly took the letter and put it in her purse.

"Here are a few pictures he had taken when he was at Westover Air Force Base."

Molly started looking through them. There was a picture of Helina's mother with Warren.

"I can't believe my eyes! The airman that Helina's mother was so crazy about was Warren. This is like a dream, Gary! I can't believe I was so close and never knew! Wait until I tell Helina. She won't believe it! Her mother will be sad to hear that he has died. I guess I wasn't supposed to meet him, but now I do know what he looked like."

Gary looked at Molly, then looked at the picture of Warren.

"You do look a little like him. I know this is a lot to take in, Molly. Are you sure you are all right?"

"Yes, I am fine. I am so glad I got to meet you, Mrs. Evans."

"So am I, Molly. I hope we can get to know each other."

"That would be nice. You are my only grandchild, Molly, and I didn't know if I would ever get to meet you. But I prayed that someday you would come."

Mrs. Evans started to cry again.

"Please, don't cry."

"Warren wanted so much to know you. He said he dreamed about you all the time."

"Well, that made two of us. I dreamed about him, and I didn't even know what he looked like. I would get so far and then the dream would stop. It was torture. I knew that I had to find out about him."

"I am so glad you came. You have an aunt that lives down the road. She's Warren's younger sister. Her name is Evelyn. I don't know how she will take meeting you. She is still grieving Warren's death really bad. She didn't like your mother. She always tried to tell Warren what to do. I think that was one of the reasons he stayed in the Air Force for twenty years."

"So, he never married?"

"No, he always said your mother was the only woman he loved. Do you want to go up to Evelyn's house and meet her?"

Molly was quiet for a minute. The door opened and in walked a tall thin blonde woman. Mrs. Evans got up and said, "Evelyn, look who is here. It's Molly, Warren's daughter and her husband, Gary."

Evelyn looked straight at Molly and said, "So, your mother told you he died, and you came to see what you could get?"

Molly stood up fast and said, "No, I came to find his grave. I was told he died in 1946, before I was born. Your mother has told me what I wanted to know. I want nothing from you."

Gary got up and said, "Come on, Molly. We are leaving."

Mrs. Evans said, "Please, Molly. Evelyn doesn't mean what she said. She is out of her mind with grief. Here, take my address. Please write me and let me know what is going on in your life. I am an old lady and my life is about over. I would love to get to know you."

"Thank you for showing me Warren's picture."

"Here, take this one. You at least deserve that."

"Thank you, Mrs. Evans. I will write to you."

Gary and Molly went out the door. Molly looked back as they were backing out of the driveway. She saw her grandmother standing there, clutching Warren's picture up next to her heart. She knew she was crying. Gary looked over at Molly. "You made that very sad woman very happy. She lost her son, but she found her granddaughter."

"Yes, but there are so many unanswered questions. Oh, I've got that letter."

"Read your letter, Molly. Maybe that will be your answer."

Molly took the letter out of her purse and began to read it:

Dear Molly,

I don't know if you will ever read this or not, but I have been in the bedroom for a couple days by myself talking to the Lord. I know my time has come to leave this world. My heart is so heavy. I know God has forgiven me for the wrong I did, but I will never know if you have. I am so sorry. I hope you can find it in your heart to forgive me. I know you have had a wonderful life. I know Mr. Preston is a great father. I wrote him once, but I am sure he probably tore up the note. I know he loved you and your mother. I stayed out of your life because I promised your mother. I did see you a few times from a distance. I have always loved you, Molly. A day has never gone by that I didn't regret what I did. I hope you will get to know your grandmother. She is a wonderful person. She will tell you whatever you want to know. And when you meet my sister Evelyn, you will probably understand why I stayed in the Air Force for twenty years. She always tried to run my life. She kept telling me not to marry your mother. I should have been a stronger man and not listened to her, but I can't go back. I can just hope you will forgive me.

Warren

Molly just looked at Gary as they drove down the road.

"How sad he must have been. He did love me enough to stay away and let me have a good life. My heart is so sad for him. It is okay, because at least I did get to see him. I didn't know it was Warren, but God let me see him. So I think in a way, I finally have opened my dream. Let's go home to Indiana. I have a great big wonderful family waiting on us."

THE END

To order additional copies of

UnOpen Dream

have your credit card ready and call
From USA: (800) 917-BOOK (2665)
From Canada: (877) 855-6732

or e-mail
orders@selahbooks.com

or order online at
www.selahbooks.com